# OFF ☆ BASE

TESSA BAILEY
SOPHIE JORDAN

everafterROMANCE

Cover design by Kim Killion of The Killion Group.

ISBN: 978-1-940941-74-5

# CONTENTS

To Kelli,

# BECK & KENNA

## TESSA BAILEY

Thank you for being such a supportive presence and valued reader.

Enjoy Beck ♡

Love, Tessa Bailey xo

# CHAPTER ONE

*All hail the world's shittiest welcoming committee.*

Kenna Sutton sat at the stoplight, chipped red nails drumming on the steering wheel. *Come on. Change.* She could feel the car full of soldiers to her left trying to get her attention. On a typical day, she would rev the engine of her baby blue Dodge Challenger, invite them to a race they would inevitably lose. But she was late—*painfully* late—to pick up one of their brethren. A soldier returning this morning from a staggering six years overseas, whose family was apparently too busy to greet him. So how had this landed on her shoulders? Just another perk of being Lieutenant General Sutton's daughter.

"Forget this," she muttered, stamping her foot down on the accelerator and screeching through the red light. Only one mile to go until she reached the landing zone. This last-minute favor to her father might be a pain in the ass, but she refused to let him down. She'd already done enough letting down to last a lifetime, and it was rare that he entrusted her with anything of importance, so she wouldn't screw it up. Too badly.

Her knowledge of the man she'd been tasked with transporting to the barracks began and ended with one fact: he was some kind of strategic mastermind. Well, that wasn't entirely true. She knew his name and rank. Major Beck Collier's skill set must be something special, because he'd made himself indispensable to the Army. Six years' worth of indispensable. And not one familiar face to latch on to when he landed.

Kenna swallowed the unexpected wave of sympathy and took a hard right, smiling as her tires squealed. The only benefit to waking up at the crack of dawn to pick up the stuffed-shirt geekster she envisioned was a chance to drive her baby. Listen to the engine purr like a contented leopard. With a wave of troops returning home, the winding roads of Fort Black Rock shouldn't have been empty, which meant the visitors were already at the site. *Dammit.*

She slowed down just in time to prevent bottoming out as she pulled into the parking lot. The first available space she saw was at the very perimeter of the lot, but she was way too late to be choosey. Seconds after she threw the Challenger into park, she'd snatched up her makeshift sign that simply read *Collier*, and was jogging across the parking lot, her heavy Dirty Laundry combat boots pounding on the asphalt.

*Running on a Sunday. Fucking obscene.*

Car windows had been decorated with painted flags and the names of soldiers in big, bold letters. *Welcome Home!* In the distance, she could hear a marching band playing "God Bless America," making her slow to a walk. The Fort Black Rock marching band was notoriously terrible, and the longer she put off being in their vicinity, the better.

A uniformed guard stopped her at the chain-link fence. "Need to see your identification, ma'am."

*He must be new.* That wasn't arrogance talking, although God knew she had a healthy dose of the stuff. She'd lived on base since birth and people—namely men—tended to know her. They didn't call her a cocktease behind her back for blending in, did they? With a sigh, she tugged the wallet from her back pocket and tossed it to the guard, popping a stick of mint gum into her mouth as he looked it over. She knew the exact moment he recognized her last name because his eyebrows disappeared into his helmet. "I'm sorry, Miss Sutton. Go right in."

"You're a gem." Kenna walked into the airfield, pushing her wallet back into the pocket of her jeans as she went. A group of photographers and journalists blocked her view at first, but as soon as she breached the human wall they'd created, she saw the soldiers disembarking from the plane. Men carrying Army-green duffel bags over their shoulders strode into the arms of crying women. Babies were kissed. Photos were taken. Proposals were made on bended knee. It was enough to warm the blackest of hearts. Even hers, apparently.

Feeling the odd spark in her chest, Kenna looked away quickly, wincing as the marching band struck up their awkward rendition of "Wild Blue Yonder." Wasn't that song reserved for the Air Force? Holding the homemade sign above her suddenly aching head, she made her way to the greeting area, scoping the sea of soldiers for an older gentleman by himself. Strategic masterminds probably wore thick-rimmed glasses, had pasty skin...maybe a slight paunch from too many hours in front of a computer, right? The second she dropped him off at the barracks, he'd probably dive on the first available video game controller. Didn't matter to her. She'd already be back in bed, finishing her Sunday the way she'd originally intended. Counting sheep.

"Excuse me, ma'am," a gravelly voice said behind her. "Are you my ride?"

Before she turned around to face the *second* guy to ma'am her in less than five minutes, intuition started to creep in. Little prickles danced on the back of her neck as she pivoted. And locked eyes on the broadest chest she'd ever seen. It was easily as wide as two of her, and then some. The patch on his right pec read *Collier*. *No way*. She tilted her head back…and back…straight up into twin blue beacons of *yes, please*. His eyes outshone the sky outlining his shaved dark-blond head. Put it to shame.

*What are you now, a poet? Get your jaw off the floor.*

Kenna hated surprises unless she was the one delivering them. She'd been expecting someone who might have a poster of Neil deGrasse Tyson on his wall. Instead, she'd gotten an NFL quarterback. He might have been a linebacker, if it weren't for his distinct All-American, good-ol'-boy, Kenny Chesney-listening, Levi's-wearing, mama's-home-cooking-eating vibe. It was louder than the goddamn marching band.

"Depends." She let her gaze drop to his tree-trunk-sized thighs under the pretense of adjusting her sunglasses. "Are you Major Beck Collier?"

His grin was a mile wide. "At your service, ma'am."

Good god. What was that accent? Georgia? Definitely the south. "Look, dude. Anytime you want to stop *ma'am*-ing me would be swell."

Smile slipping, he nodded as if she'd imparted life-saving instructions. "Is there something I can call you instead?"

Hold the phone. This guy didn't even know her name. Which meant…he didn't know she was Lieutenant General Sutton's daughter? When walking around base, she might as well wear a flashing neon sign that said *looky no touchy*. And oh, they *looked*. She made sure of it. But on the rare occasion a man actually approached, he was clued in pronto about whose loins she'd sprung forth from. Kenna had no intention of taking advantage of True Blue, being that he was the furthest thing from her type as one could get. But at least she wouldn't be treated like *Kenna, Spawn of Sutton*, throughout the drive.

"I'm Kenna. Welcome back and whatnot." Suddenly at a loss without her name to precede her, she gestured to the canvas bag on the ground. "Do you need help with that?"

His expression was one of horror. "No, ma'am—*Kenna*. I can manage." He shifted on his size-nine-hundred feet. "Do you need help with anything?"

She looked around. "Like what? Walking?"

Unbelievable. This handsome, hulking man actually turned a little red. "Just in general, I guess." He gave a little head shake. "You'll have to pardon me. I haven't been around a woman for a while. You caught me a little off guard, is all. I didn't expect—"

"Expect what?"

He appeared to be struggling with the effort to keep his gaze above her neck. Which was a huge feat, considering she wore a leather bustier and skintight, low-rise jeans that left several inches of her belly exposed. Honestly, her boobs were looking at *him*. Anyone with a penis should have returned the favor by now and usually did. Without fail. His Adam's apple slid up and down. "Can we start over?"

"Nope. What didn't you expect?"

Beck's blue eyes fell to hers, then looked away again. Anywhere but *at* her. "I guess I..." He cleared his throat. "I didn't expect my ride to be so beautiful she makes my stomach hurt. I didn't expect that." He ducked his head and breezed past her, toward the parking lot, while Kenna stood frozen to the pavement.

• • •

*Five minutes back on US soil and you've already made a jackass out of yourself.*

Beck hefted his bag higher on his shoulder, refusing to acknowledge the pain that ripped through his right side. Or maybe he *should* acknowledge it. Focus in on the wound's discomfort, let it spread down to his toes. It might take his mind off the girl he could hear jogging to catch up with him. Should she really be jogging in that shirt? Could one even *call* it a shirt?

*Mind your manners.* Beck slowed down until they were walking side by side, but kept his gaze resolutely on the parking lot ahead. Didn't it figure the good Lord would test him the moment he landed? He'd been warned the transition back to civilian life wouldn't be easy. Learning how to grocery shop, buying sneakers, eating at Denny's. He could—*would*—handle those things. But five tempting feet of female curves and attitude? No, sir. Beck wasn't quite ready for that.

For the first time, he regretted not asking his twin

sister, Huntley—a nurse on base—to pick him up. Or his best friend, Cullen, who worked on base training soldiers in explosives and demolition. Both of them would have dropped everything at a moment's notice. He'd just needed some time. Time to wrap his mind around being home for the first time in six years. Time to prepare himself for the news he would impart. Time to accept that everything had changed.

Kenna's smoky incense scent might as well have been a wrench twisting in his gut. He didn't have firsthand knowledge of what those ancient gypsy women who sold magic smelled like, but he reckoned it was similar to Kenna. The keyword being *similar*, because he somehow knew her scent couldn't be replicated on another woman.

*Listen to yourself. What do you know about women?*

For the last year, he'd been locked inside a command center full of high-ranking officers, field scientists, journalists. Before that? Well, he'd been waiting. Would *still* be waiting, if there was anything left to wait for back home in Georgia.

They reached the parking lot and Beck immediately moved behind Kenna, guiding her without touching through the moving sea of cars. From this position, he could pull her back if a vehicle moved too fast. Touching would be required for that, though, so he prayed it wasn't necessary. Or was he praying for the exact opposite? *Don't look at her backside.*

She threw a look at him over her shoulder, green eyes glowing just above the rim of her sunglasses. "You in a rush to be somewhere, Major?"

*Home. So I can get rid of this pain in my stomach.* This wasn't his home, though. It was only temporary.

"No rush." He followed her lead down the last row of

cars, watching as she sent the sign bearing his name fluttering into a metal garbage can. "I figure you have somewhere you'd rather be than chauffeuring me around base."

Kenna stopped at the trunk of a blue Challenger—a beaut, to be sure—and turned to face him. "I'm a firm believer that Sundays should be spent in bed. Don't you agree?"

Beck lassoed the groan trying to break free from his throat, yanking it back. The thought of her tossing around in tangled sheets...

Enough. This girl was doing him a kindness, and his mind could only muster inappropriate thoughts. Someone who looked, moved and spoke like her was probably on the receiving end of such thoughts on a regular basis. He wouldn't repeat the pattern, although intuition told Beck she wanted him to. "I tend to agree, Kenna." He nodded once. "You should always take the opportunity to catch up on sleep. Sleep is nature's reset button."

A laugh bubbled from her lips. "You aren't going to fit in here, True Blue."

The husky endearment made the wrench below his belt tighten. "It's a good thing I don't intend to be here long then."

For some reason, his response seemed to remind her of something. She stepped toward the car, digging in her front pocket to pull out a jingling set of car keys. The action tugged the denim low—*way* too low—giving him a glimpse at the barbed wire tattoo circling her hips and the edge of sheer black panties. Beck's mouth went dry as the desert he'd returned from. And just when he thought it couldn't get any worse, she popped the trunk and lifted it. Her stomach muscles stretched, the shirt—was it even a shirt?—gliding up her taut stomach and tightening over her high breasts.

Beck swung the bag off his shoulder and held it over his lap before she could witness his reaction to her body. His hard-on was becoming a serious problem. It wouldn't go away as long as Kenna was in the vicinity, and they still had the car ride to get through.

"Throw your bag in the trunk."

"No, thanks. I think I'll hang on to it."

She lifted an eyebrow. "The passenger side of my car will barely fit you, let alone all your earthly possessions."

"If you don't mind, I'll try and make do."

With a shrug, she slammed the trunk and headed for the driver's side door. Letting loose a relieved breath, he made his way to the opposite side. Keeping the bag in place with one arm, he opened the passenger door and immediately admitted she'd been right. Barely enough room for him and his bag. Not to mention the vicious wood he was sporting. Seeing no other choice, he dropped down into the seat, wedging the canvas bag between his thighs, the leather upholstery groaning beneath him as he did so.

He looked over at Kenna to find her battling a smile. "Seatbelt."

"Heck."

With considerable effort, he managed to wrap the strap around himself and the bag as Kenna watched with open amusement from the driver's side. Once the belt clicked into place, she threw her right arm over his seat and started to back out of the parking spot. Beck caught a glimpse of her straining breasts and decided it best to stare up at the ceiling, but not before his erection grew swollen enough to steal oxygen from his lungs.

They exited the parking lot and turned onto the road. "So," she said. "What did you miss most while you were gone, Major?"

Beck answered honestly, even though concentration was difficult. "My sister; she's a nurse here on base. My dog, Moses. Buttered popcorn from the movie theater. My mother down in Georgia. Not in that exact order, mind you. My mother rates higher than popcorn."

"I hope so." She adjusted the air conditioner, not that he could feel it as his bag blocked the vent. Too bad, he could use cooling down. "You're headed back to Georgia?"

"Yes, ma'am. *Kenna*," he corrected himself. "Peach farming."

"Huh-what?"

He smiled at her confused expression, relieved she'd given him something to think about besides his wayward anatomy. "My family has been in the peach farming business for six generations. I'll be taking over operations from my grandfather. Soon as I make my way down south."

"Peaches," she murmured. "Peaches, a dog, mama and popcorn. If you tell me you don't have a girl waiting for you back in Georgia, Major, I won't believe you."

His neck grew hot, an uncomfortable pit yawning wide in his stomach. "There's no girl." That wasn't entirely true. There *had* been a girl at one time, but there wasn't any longer. And while he didn't feel the same regret he once had over it—heck, remembering her face got harder over time—discussing it in front of Kenna would only lead to pity. Embarrassment. Two things he didn't want to feel from anyone, let alone this gorgeous, confident girl who'd probably never faced a single challenge in the romance department.

Beck could see her need to press battling with her nonchalance. "You sure about that?"

He started to say *yes, he was sure*, but he stopped himself. Since that day a year ago when he'd received the Dear John letter from back home, he'd unburdened himself to no one. Today marked a fresh start, away from the pressures he'd faced overseas and the tragedy he'd been living with on his conscience. Life after his service. While he might have mentally moved on in most aspects, the failure still sat heavily on his shoulders and he wanted to be free of it. Once Kenna dropped him off, she'd probably speed away, his name flying out the window of her muscle car along with his sob story. He eyed her. What was the worst that could happen? She pretended to be sympathetic and race back to her boyfriend?

Sweet Jesus, he didn't like the idea of her crawling back into those sheets with a boyfriend.

The unexpected flare of jealousy propelled the truth out of him. "Mary was my high school girlfriend. We'd been going together since freshman year, followed each other to the University of North Georgia. Everything was fine, until I took the ASVAB test." He still recalled being summoned out of class to discuss his unusually high results on the military aptitude test with a recruiter. "After that, everything happened so fast. I was shipped out before the ink dried."

"I know the test." She measured him with a look. "That explains how you've been promoted to major so young."

"All due respect, Kenna, twenty-six isn't young when you've been where I have." He barely managed to keep his gaze from dropping to her parted thighs on the seat. "Speaking of, how old are you?"

Her grin was pure mischief. "Twenty-two." Oh no. This

girl was too young to be lusting after, wasn't she? As if she could sense the direction of his thoughts, she hauled him back to the present. "Tell me about Mary."

He swallowed, unable to believe he was sharing the story out loud. "Mary was the pastor's daughter in our town. We were…she was…waiting. For me." He waved a hand. "And then she didn't."

Kenna pursed her lips. "Like, waiting until you came home to get married?"

Had he turned green? He felt green. "Yes, for marriage and…waiting in general. For other things. We both were."

He saw the moment everything clicked into place. Her eyes widened. Yup. She was transporting a virgin. A cuckolded one at that. "Oh. Oh, wow." She was silent a full minute. "So Mary—oh God, the *Virgin Mary*—was waiting for you to come home, so she could give you her…flower… but someone else plucked it. Do I follow?"

"That's about right." He could see the barracks in the distance, telling him the ride was almost over. Half of him was relieved, the other half oddly nervous about her leaving.

"When did you find out Mary had done that to you?"

"She sent the letter about a year ago, although it might have been going on longer. I don't know."

Kenna pursed her lips. "Most men wouldn't have wasted any time finding out what they'd been missing." She slid him a glance. "Why not you?"

"I'd already waited nearly a decade, I figured one more year wouldn't kill me. Especially when there were men and women fighting for their lives and losing every single day." Men like his childhood friend, Xander, who Beck had sent on his final mission. "What did I have to complain about, you know? There might have been opportunities if I'd looked for them, but I didn't want to. It felt wrong."

Beck was surprised to see they'd pulled up in front of the barracks. Kenna looked a little shocked herself as she shifted the car into park. "I'm sorry. Finding out in a letter… that really shouldn't have happened to someone like you."

"Hey." He sent her a half grin, hoping to dispel the heaviness he'd created in the car. It was suddenly important he not leave her with a negative impression of their short time together. "I'm here on solid ground, ain't I? Living and breathing. That's more than a lot of soldiers can say." Beck took one last look at her pretty face, memorizing her upturned top lip, wishing he could get one last peek at the glowing green eyes hidden behind her sunglasses. Her stubborn chin. It felt wrong to leave her, but what choice did he have? She wouldn't very well want to date the pathetic, betrayed virgin he'd revealed himself to be. Even if she did, he only had four days at Black Rock before flying back to Georgia. "Goodbye, Kenna." He scratched the back of his neck. "I must have done something right along the way to earn a ride from such a pretty girl, huh? You take care now."

A lump stuck in his throat as he heaved his bag through the door and climbed out of the car.

# CHAPTER TWO

*What the ever-loving fuck just happened?*

Kenna stared out the windshield of her car, watching Beck climb the concrete stairs leading to his home for—how long? A day? A month? They hadn't gotten around to the particulars of his stay. There'd been no real small talk, had there? No, he'd bared it all in the span of ten minutes. Just *do not pass go...do not gawk at the magnificent virgin in the passenger's seat.* Because as she watched him move with a mixture of unassuming grace and innate confidence, she could freely admit that yes, he was indeed magnificent. The set of his shoulders, the sturdiness of him said this was a man who moved mountains if he put his mind to it.

No, there was no *if* about it. He *had.* Or at least he'd managed to shift something mountain-like inside her in a mere ten minutes. What was she supposed to do with these sucky, yucky feelings? Just watch him disappear into the barracks, effectively letting him get away with it? People—men, especially—usually took one look at her stormtrooper-meets-Cyndi Lauper look and wasted no time lobbing innuendoes at her head like mud-covered softballs. She never cared because those dudes all blurred together in a rippling sea of douchebags. This guy wouldn't *blend.* He'd confided in her, and she was heavy with that responsibility. She…liked being heavy with that responsibility, which made no damn sense.

At the top step, Beck turned his head, catching her gaze through the windshield. She would go to her grave thankful that no one was in the car to hear the noise that left her mouth. It went something like *ohhhnooowhuu.* If he'd managed to keep the entreaty from those intense blue eyes, she might have driven off and endeavored to forget about Major Beck Collier, virgin extraordinaire. But it was there, even if he didn't realize it. He needed someone. Someone kind and compassionate. That someone definitely wasn't her, but he sure as shit needed *someone*, and there was no one else around.

She watched him tug a single key from his canvas bag and open the door. He ducked beneath the doorframe and vanished a second later. Kenna didn't realize her fingers were digging into the steering wheel until they started to hurt. A sense of urgency danced in her ribcage, fluttering rapidly, slowly climbing into her throat.

"Goddammit." She swiped a hand through her dark, messy hair before pushing open the driver's side door and stepping out.

The morning chill had begun to dissipate, the ground soaking up the minimal heat and reflecting it onto her denim-clad legs. This parking lot was usually buzzing by now, but the Sunday silence amplified the sound of her boots clomping along the asphalt, echoing the nervous knocking inside her ribcage. On the second floor, she could see Beck had left the door slightly ajar, almost as if he'd hoped she'd follow. *Please let that be the case.* Otherwise this move was a smidge on the creepy side. She'd only signed on to be his transport, not his kick-it buddy.

*Decision is already made, Kenna.* Too bad she didn't have a clue what she would do once they were in the apartment together. She had no game plan. Or exit strategy. But she knew driving away would feel awful if she didn't do *something*, so she followed in his footsteps up the stairs, like one of those cartoon characters floating along on the aroma of fresh-baked apple pie. Or peach pie, as it were.

"Hardy har," Kenna muttered, stopping outside the door. Since when did she hesitate to do anything? To celebrate her eighteenth birthday, she'd gone streaking at the annual Army/Navy football game. Scaled the local water tower, spray-painting *Kenna was here...with beer* on the side. As a welder, she worked with fire, for fuck sake. Being nervous around a virgin was flat-out unacceptable. Even if he was Bigfoot-sized. After a full-body shake to loosen her nerves, she pushed the door open. When she saw Beck, her chest squeezed so tight, she swore it was wringing itself dry.

He stood still in the center of the dim, dull, undecorated apartment, bag at his feet. His hands were propped on his hips, head tipped forward. Lonely. He looked so lonely. The wrongness of that rose like an angry tide over her and immediately, she had a game plan.

Although, it felt nothing like a game.

Kenna squared her shoulders and breezed into the apartment, beelining for the kitchen. If someone hadn't stocked the place with basic food staples for this man, she was going to raise hell next time she saw her father. "I decided to hang out for a while, Major. You're welcome." She tugged open the refrigerator door, pleased to see a loaf of bread, butter, cheese. A six-pack. "You hungry?"

She didn't wait for his answer, but started piling ingredients onto the counter. Thank God she had something to do with her hands because after a full minute, Beck still hadn't answered. Bad move. This had been a *bad* move. For all she knew, he had plans. Or—

"Kenna."

His gruff voice came from right behind her and the fluttering in her ribcage moved lower, so she didn't turn around in case it showed in her expression. "Yeah?"

"You don't have to do this. I can make myself a sandwich."

"You shouldn't have to." She threw a pack of Kraft singles hard onto the counter and crossed her arms. "Someone should be here to welcome you back. It's not right."

The stretch of silence was driving her crazy, so she turned to face him...and forgot how to inhale. Starved. He looked starved for something other than food. His pupils had swallowed the blue of his eyes, throat working up and down, even as he kept his gaze determinedly above her neck. Who *was* this man?

"It was my choice," he said. "My choice not to burden anyone. Not just yet."

Kenna took a step closer, and he sucked in a breath. God, the effect she was having on him...it thrilled her, made her legs go weak, but at the same time she felt his acute pain. Frustration. "You don't seem like the type to be a burden," she muttered. "The exact opposite, actually."

"I appreciate you saying so." There it was. He slipped. His attention falling to her breasts for the barest of seconds before racing back up. When he spoke again, his jaw was so tight, she could hardly understand him. "But it ain't true. What I came back with, what I failed to do...it'll be a burden on everyone soon enough."

Curiosity demanded she question him, but his words stopped her. She was the queen of avoidance and understood his need to delay the inevitable. Whatever it was. She also knew exactly how to distract him from thoughts of being a burden. It was why she'd followed him upstairs, wasn't it? Yes, she could admit that now. Admit to this irrefutable need to smooth his frayed edges, to make up for the betrayal he'd experienced. It was this man inspiring the need to provide solace. No one else could have done it.

Kenna reached down and took his hand, leading him from the kitchen. As they passed through the brown-on-gray living room, she scowled, hating the dust motes in the air. The lack of character. She knew the moment Beck realized she was leading him to the bedroom because his breath began rattling in and out behind her. His hand tightened around hers as if he wanted to pull her to a stop, but couldn't find the will. When they cleared the threshold, Kenna let go of his hand and kicked the door shut.

He shook his head as she toed off her boots and slowly approached. "W-what are you doing?"

She pushed him into a sitting position on the bed, raked her fingers up his massive thighs. "I'm welcoming you home, Major."

* * *

Beck reached deep inside himself, searching for the extra slack in his rope. *Can't find it. Can't.* He'd reached the end. Resisting her might have been possible before she'd touched his legs, but no one had ever touched him there on purpose. Not so close to his dick. Christ above, was she going to touch him *there*? He held his breath, head falling back on his shoulders as her touch inched higher, higher. *Please touch me. Grab me hard.*

Just before she reached his lap, her hands detoured up the front of his uniform jacket. Beck released a shaky exhale and she laughed softly. Knowingly? When she reached the top, he tipped his head forward again to watch her undo the buttons. One by one, she popped them open, green eyes steady on him as she worked. His severe disappointment that she hadn't touched his throbbing erection gave way to awe. What was this gorgeous, electric girl doing here with him? Her face was mere inches from his, her mouth so ripe. So delicious looking, while at the same time a little...bad. The kind of mouth he dreamed about at night, alone in his bunk as he stroked himself off. He shouldn't be thinking of her—parts of her—as an object. What was wrong with him?

*Hot. I'm so hot. Need more than my own hand. Nothing is working anymore.*

Kenna pushed the jacket off his shoulders and down, leaving his hands tangled in the sleeves at his back. He started to free his hands, but she stayed him with a head shake. "Major?"

"Yeah?" He swallowed hard. "Yes?"

She moved closer between his outstretched thighs,

stroking her nails over his shaved head. It felt so damn good, he moaned. A moan cut off by what she said next. "You can look at my body."

As if magnetized, his hungry gaze landed on her breasts and devoured. They weren't good-girl breasts, the kind that girls of his recollection hid beneath white cardigans in church. Kenna would have been called a sinner if she'd walked into his old church, no matter what she was wearing. She didn't have breasts, she had…tits. Naughty, up-to-no-good, made-to-bounce tits. The kind he'd seen in skin magazines or in high-quality porn, when he broke down every so often and watched. They were pushed up in leather, exactly as they were meant to be. Heck, if he tugged her top down a mere inch, her nipple would pop free. The thought of licking her little peaks while she sat on his thighs sent another bolt of uncomfortable lust straight to his dick, forcing him to shift on the bed.

"Kenna, I've never seen anything like you," he ground out. "But I can't look anymore or I'll embarrass myself."

She surprised him by leaning in and kissing the corner of his mouth. "Nothing you do or say here will be embarrassing."

Then she dropped to her knees. Beck's cock surged against his fly with such intensity, his hands untangled themselves from his jacket with frantic movements so he could grip his aching length. He had no choice…would have done anything to ease the agonizing throb. His gaze shot to hers, dreading the judgment he'd find there as he squeezed and released. Stroked through his restricting pants. These uncontrollable urges of his had become too much. No matter how often he denied them, they never stopped, only gaining intensity. He witnessed no judgment on her face. Instead, he saw pleasure. Seduction. She liked watching him touch himself? Jesus…she *did*.

Beck found himself widening his thighs and leaning back on one elbow so she could watch. Just having her attention centered there was going to be enough to finish him. More. More. Just a little more. But before he could start that final ascent, she removed his hand, replacing it with her own. His elbow gave out and he fell back on the bed, thighs shaking, stomach clenching.

"Have you ever had a woman's mouth here, Major?"

"No," he croaked. "Please. I know I shouldn't ask, but *please*. I'll do anything."

He forced himself to lift his head so he could watch her unfasten his belt, work his button, unzip his fly. The lessening of pressure wrenched a groan from his throat, but nothing on his earth would ever compare to seeing his stiff dick in her grip. The softness of a woman's—no, not just a woman… Kenna's—hands put his own to shame. Precum leaked from the tip the first time she stroked her fist from base to head as his chest shuddered in and out on harsh breaths.

"She missed out, didn't she, sweetheart?" She looked up at him under heavy eyelids. "You're going to make some woman very happy with this."

Her pink tongue skated over the tip, and his hips jerked wildly on the bed. "Darlin'. Darlin', please…I'm hurting. I'm hurting all over." Jesus, he'd never called anyone darlin' in his life and who the hell cared? He reached down and wound a fist in her hair because he couldn't *not* use her as an anchor. "Is this okay?"

"Hold on tight," she whispered, before sucking half of

his erection into her mouth. Beck shouted the vilest of curses at the ceiling. Swore his life was coming to an end. Every ounce of feeling in his body raced to his already sensitive cock, swelling it inside the sweet heat of her mouth. That mouth, that *mouth* that was designed for sinning, hummed around him as it worked, the vibrations hitting his balls like lightning strikes. Savoring noises that polarized and woke a beast inside of him at the same time. His survival was in Kenna's control, and he gave it over without a moment's hesitation, trusting her to end the torment. In that moment, she was everything. His sin, his salvation, his caretaker. All of it.

"Your mouth. God, your mouth. You. Just you, Kenna. I've needed you so bad."

Every last thought bled from his mind when she took him to the back of her throat. She beat him off with several quick strokes as she sucked back to the tip and his very consciousness wavered. Nothing had ever felt this unbelievable. Nothing. It didn't seem real, yet it was the most tangible thing he'd ever experienced. Never stop. Never.

"*Keep doing that.* Suck, just suck it hard for me. The way I've been dreaming." His fists tightened in her hair. "Please, Kenna, *please.* Again, again. I'm going to—"

Beck broke off with a roar as blinding pleasure ripped through his middle. He lost control of his body, hips pumping upward trying to wring every last glimmer of perfection from Kenna's mouth. Her fingernails dug into his thighs and she moaned around him, taking everything he had and more. The more he hadn't known existed until now. The pain in his stomach faded into a dull memory, muscles practically liquefying him onto the mattress. It was impossible to wrap his mind around the stunning relief, so he scooped Kenna off the floor and onto his lap and held her, inhaling her incense scent in greedy gulps, knowing he would equate it with pleasure for the rest of his life and he was glad for it.

But the sweeping relief vanished when he became aware of her movements. She shifted in his lap, hands clenching and unclenching in the material of his shirt. "Now *you*, Kenna," he growled, tipping her flushed face up. "Show me how to do that for you."

Her nod was jerky, gaze refusing to find his. "When we wake up, okay?"

Sleep? He couldn't sleep knowing she was experiencing the same discomfort he'd been afflicted with. Not a chance. "No. I need you better." Hoping he wasn't going too far, Beck pushed her thighs open, wincing at her moan. "Oh God, please...let me take care of it. My hands, my mouth—"

"No," she blurted, softening her refusal by rubbing circles onto his chest. "I'm not *ready* just yet, okay?"

She seemed ready to him—*beyond* ready—but he'd rather saw off his arm than push a woman toward anything she didn't want. Even if the idea of leaving her wanting sort of felt like both arms had already been sawed clean off. Dammit, he should *know* what to do here. How to fix her. It hurt to swallow. "When we wake up?"

"Yes," she breathed. He reclined back onto the mattress, taking her body with him. He swore there was no way in hell he'd fall asleep, but then, he'd never had Kenna curled up underneath his arm. Never had her rub her face on his shoulder. Never felt her tuck her small feet between his legs.

*Home. I'm finally home.*

That was his last conscious thought before he fell asleep.

# CHAPTER THREE

Kenna stared through the lens of her helmet at the two pieces of cut metal she was welding together, but found herself getting lost in the blue sparks. She set her welding gun down and slumped onto the workshop stool. From across the space, she could feel her friend Darla watching in that quiet way that used to unnerve her, but right now only served as an irritant.

Feeling irrationally restless, she pushed her helmet up and studied the half-completed sculpture sitting ten yards away on an elevated pedestal. Yesterday, the idea of finishing the piece of artwork that would be displayed in a local park had imbued her with a sense of accomplishment, but nothing was penetrating her preoccupied state of mind today. Not even Darla, who sat perched on the adjacent workbench tracing the spine of a thick book with a single finger. Probably Tolkien. Or something else that involved a Middle Earth-like setting.

It was Monday afternoon and her friend had just broken

free of second-grade hell, hoping to catch Kenna in the workshop. As if she'd be anywhere else. These days she seemed to spend every free second in the dark workshop, working on various orders from around the country. When she wasn't chauffeuring giant, sweetly complicated men around base and subsequently giving them a sexual education, that is. Or the beginnings of one. Before she'd crept out the apartment door and burned rubber getting out of the parking lot.

Totally healthy.

She wasn't too proud to admit she'd gone home afterward, rifled through her sock drawer for the perfect vibrator, flipped it to the highest setting and gone to town. Because, holy mother of blow jobs, she hadn't even been the one receiving pleasure and yet she'd never—*never*—been hotter in her life. The way Beck had begged, twisted on the bed, yanking on her hair and gasping in such a purely masculine way, she'd shivered the entire time. Not only had lust burned her from head to toe, there had been unmistakable power. Power in being the first for him. However, something beside Beck's wood had popped up. A...connection. A passing of trust. An idea far too emotional to acknowledge, so she was hell-bent on ignoring it.

But Beck didn't want to be ignored. A day later and she still felt guilty for leaving. More than guilt, though. She couldn't shake the intuition she should have stayed.

*And done what, Kenna?* Found out more about his sweet-potato-eating, aw-shucks-ing life? The last thing she wanted was to get caught up with some peach farmer who missed his dog. They had nothing in common. Except their apparent love of getting him off.

"Oh, um. Hi over there?" Darla hopped off the workbench, clutching Tolkien to her chest. "You can't think that hard while holding a blow torch. It's a hazard, and I'm not wearing the appropriate footwear to run from a structural fire."

Kenna eyed her friend's plaid clogs, complete with metal spikes on the heel and admitted Darla was right. She'd be doomed. "Where do you even find shoes like that?"

"Don't make me explain the Internet again."

Kenna removed her helmet and ran a rag over her sweaty head. "One time. *One* time I have trouble downloading a file and I'm suddenly classified as a computer-illiterate granny."

"Nah, they teach grannies the Internet now."

They traded an exaggerated smirk. "Okay, fine. I'm done for the day. Disaster averted."

"I'll be the judge of that." Darla propped her slight hip against Kenna's workstation. "What has you thinking so hard? Saturday night we ate pizza and watched *The Hobbit*—"

"Against my will."

"—and today you've gone from Sporty Spice to Scary Spice."

"Jesus. I can't take the Spice Girls rating system today." Kenna melted off her stool and clomped toward the mini fridge for a bottle of water. How long had she been working? "I'm just bogged down with work orders. It has me stressed."

"What did you do yesterday?"

The water bottle paused in its ascent toward her mouth. Ah, the hell with it. She was too tired from her sleepless night to lie convincingly. Not to mention, her astute friend would get it out of her eventually, so this was merely a timesaver.

"Hooked up with a virgin who'd just landed back at base. Started to make him a sandwich, but, uh—"

"Yeah, right."

"What? I make the dopest sandwiches."

Darla calmly set down her hardcover book on Kenna's vacated stool. "Kenna, I've known you for four years and you've never hooked up on base. Not so much as a kiss on the cheek from a soldier." She let her words hang in the air for a beat. "You are religious about leaving base when you want male company. The whole thing with your mother—"

"Hey." Kenna laughed a little too loud. "This is getting a little deep for a Monday. Maybe I just decided to switch up the old routine. Nothing to be alarmed about."

"I'm not alarmed. I'm just surprised." Darla's red-painted mouth lifted on one side. "Who was the lucky anomaly, you sly dog?"

"Uh, you sound like a dirty old man." Kenna attempted to hide her reddening face by pulling the protective leather apron over her head. "Seriously, it doesn't matter. He's going back to Georgia and I'll never see him again. It was just a thing."

"A thing."

"Yeah." Kenna waved her hand. "A thing."

"A *virgin* thing is so *not* your thing."

Oh, yes it was. It was *so* her thing; she couldn't think about it without contemplating another run for her sock drawer. Big muscled thighs, his voice cracking, not an ounce of male bullshit. Just pure awe and gratefulness…his all-out *roar* when he came. The way he'd cradled her to his chest afterward like a precious artifact. Damn. *No thinking about that, remember?*

"Speaking of male company, we need another road trip soon." Kenna skirted past her friend and started to clean off her cluttered workbench. Darla was right. She'd broken her rule. Memories didn't fade at Black Rock and her mother's loose reputation continued to linger. Kenna got a kick out of dressing provocatively while never, *ever*, letting a single soldier lay a hand on her. Maybe it signaled her twisted sense of humor, but it was Kenna's little way of punishing them for judging her mother for behavior deemed acceptable for *men*. Yeah, she'd burned her rulebook last night. Killed it dead. Now, even making the suggestion they go to a neighboring town, far from the base gossip mill, felt somehow disloyal. And completely unappealing. Bad. Very bad. "How about tonight?"

Darla's face adopted its stern teacher countenance. "On a school night?"

"Come on—"

Kenna's cell phone vibrated in the back pocket of her jeans. She fished it out between her thumb and forefinger, read the display name and smiled. "Father. Hi."

"Kenna." His gruff, no-nonsense voice boomed down the line. "Staying out of trouble?"

Her heart sank a little. "Yes, sir."

That wasn't a lie, but she'd deserved the question. In the not-so-distant past, the lieutenant general's phone call would have gone unanswered because she would have been busy getting up to no good. *Acting out*, her school counselors had said. At the ripe old age of twenty-two, she could look back and agree. Following her parents' divorce, her mother had moved off base, which had led to Kenna being passed around every three days like a piping hot potato. She'd embraced her new role as a seeming nuisance by burdening her parents at every turn. Running away, getting picked up for public intoxication, shoplifting. It all ended five years ago when her father had a heart attack.

Something miraculous had happened. The invincible lieutenant general had begun to need her. During his recovery, Kenna had moved in permanently, become his right hand. Cooked for him, cleaned, taken him to physical therapy and administered his medication. The two of them had grown closer in their own subtle way. Although, she now wondered if her imagination had invented that bond. As soon as her father was back on his feet, she'd been sent to live with her mother. Unfortunately, by then, her mother had moved on and married her boyfriend and gotten pregnant.

Kenna had been on her own ever since. That's how she intended to keep it. Because while she loved her parents unconditionally, she knew what happened when you loved someone too much. They only loved you back until your usefulness ran out. So instead of pretending she wanted that shiny romantic future like everyone else seemed determined to have, she left base every few months, met some drunk ex-frat boy with a chip on his shoulder and engaged in a meaningless one-night stand.

It worked for her and no one got hurt.

"Glad to hear it." Her father broke back into her confidential thoughts, making Kenna cringe. *Think about puppies or unicorns.* "I need you here for dinner tonight, please. Nineteen hundred hours, on the nose. We're having a guest."

"Yes, sir," she responded tonelessly, although hearing he wanted her around filled her chest with helium. Her father might have—in essence—kicked her ass out, but that specter of the friendship they'd developed still loomed. "Do you need me to come early? I can throw something together—"

"No, thank you. Tina has it covered."

Tina. Her father's new wife. She and Kenna were cordial, but they didn't exactly exchange chatty text messages or do makeovers on each other. Apart from the day Tina had exchanged vows with the lieutenant general in their landscaped backyard, Kenna hadn't even been invited over once. Maybe that would change after dinner tonight?

"Should I bring—"

"We have everything. Just don't be late."

She nodded even though he couldn't see her. "I won't be late. See you later, sir."

When she hung up, she ignored the sympathetic look from Darla.

# CHAPTER FOUR

Beck sipped the whiskey he'd just been handed from Lieutenant General Sutton. Truth be told, he'd never much cared for spirits. The occasional beer or two during a football game seemed to fit the bill fine without hindering his ability to think, but he welcomed the unfamiliar burn of whiskey now because the taste reminded him of Kenna. If that wasn't a warning shot, he didn't know what was. The girl made him think of being drunk and out of control. Made him *want* to get that way. Who needed the ability to think when his brain seemed determined to keep her image dangling in front of his eyes like a carrot? Flashes of her sparked in front of his eyes now. The feel of her mouth, the weight of her in his lap. Pathetically, he even thought of how she'd almost made him a sandwich. He wanted to pin her down and ask her why she'd wanted to make him a sandwich. Wanted to go back in time and let her make the darn thing.

Clearly the whiskey was already taking effect.

And okay, he might have also felt the need to indulge

tonight for more than one reason. Chiefly among them, the lieutenant general had invited him for dinner, wanting to congratulate him for his role in the evacuation of five Army POWs. Scouting their location, placing surveillance on the makeshift prison, leading the extraction, despite the mission being compromised by a major explosion. He didn't want to be honored. Didn't want to be patted on the back for a job well done when he'd lost a good man on the very same mission. He banished the vision of Xander and locked out the upcoming meeting with Cullen where he would have to relate news details he wanted only to forget.

Beck shifted to ease the pressure on his right side, as if the throbbing had grown worse because of the memories. Like a lifeline, he drew Kenna's face to the forefront once more. Why? Why would he put himself through the torture when she'd left him? Lord, he'd made a fool of himself in front of her. Begging, pulling on her pretty hair. Having no idea if he should touch her to make her stop writhing around on his thigh. She'd probably laughed her way out the door when he'd fallen asleep. Had she gone back to a boyfriend? Girls who looked and smelled and made sandwiches like her had boyfriends.

When he realized his hand had tightened on the tumbler of whiskey with enough force to shatter it, he took a deep breath and loosened his grip. Lord, this aggression wasn't like him. His cool head had been a factor in earning him so many promotions. What was it about this girl?

While they waited for the final guest to arrive, Lieutenant General Sutton was relating a story of his time on the ground during the Gulf War, speaking in the hushed tones people reserved for tales of ghosts and battle. Beck's mind struggled to distance itself, find a quiet place a million miles away from thoughts of where he'd just returned from, but he wanted to be respectful, so he forced himself to pay attention to every word.

"We didn't know it at the time, but we were the lucky ones." Sutton slapped him on the back. "Same as you. Lucky enough to be alive with the life education most men aren't privy to. It'll serve you well, whether you know it or not."

Beck nodded once. "Thank you, sir. I—"

"Sorry, I'm late." A muffled female voice, followed by familiar booted footsteps, came from the front entryway, and Beck's body went screaming into high alert. All five senses sharpened the way they did before going into battle, his shoulders bracing for impact. He was experiencing déjà vu, not because his subconscious was rerunning this scene. No, because he'd *expected* it. Maybe not this exact way, but he'd expected to see her again. Would have gone to find her himself, if necessary.

Kenna was the final dinner guest? But they were waiting for Sutton's daughter. Beck felt sucker-punched as reality dawned. Kenna—the girl who'd gotten on her knees and pleasured him—was Lieutenant General Sutton's daughter. For the love of God.

He thought he'd readied himself for Kenna to walk into the room, but he'd been ten kinds of wrong. No, she strode into view in combat boots and a miniskirt, long hair—hair he'd *pulled*—piled on top of her head. And he just managed to catch himself before staggering back. It couldn't be typical, this impact she had on him. Like ten smooth sets of hands stroking over his body at the same time. He shouldn't be anxious to get those green eyes on him. Shouldn't regret he hadn't thrown her onto that damn bed yesterday, given her the kind of fucking he ached to dole out. The kind he'd watched on his laptop screen, where the female grew sweaty and moaned for the man to thrust harder, her ass shaking with the impact. No, he definitely shouldn't be thinking about that. If anything, he should be mad as all hell that she'd omitted her identity, but he couldn't muster it around the relief of seeing her again.

She was busy digging in a grocery bag and hadn't looked up yet, so he used the time to straighten up, pull himself together. Glue his gaze above her neck where it belonged, especially with her father standing at his shoulder. Jesus.

"I swear, I left right on time, but I—" Kenna looked up and the smile froze on her face. So she hadn't known either. Well, at least he wasn't the only one being caught off guard. With an obvious effort, she turned her attention to Sutton. "I, uh…s-stopped to get that beef jerky you're always going on about. The one—"

"Thank you. Although, Tina picked it up for me this morning." Sutton patted his daughter on the shoulder, much like he'd done to Beck. "I'd rather you'd been on time."

"Ah, you know me. Unfashionably late." She dropped the grocery bag down to her side, throwing a glance at Beck. "Just ask Major Collier. If I'd been any later to pick him up yesterday, he would've started walking." She widened her eyes slightly. "Right, Major?"

Beck hid his surprise that she'd acknowledged their *acquaintance* in a sip of whiskey. "I was grateful to have a ride at all on short notice. Thanks again, ma'am."

"That's right. I forgot you two already know each other," Sutton said, just as Tina joined them in the living room to take Beck's now-empty glass and sail back toward the kitchen. Beck noticed she'd only offered a passing nod in Kenna's direction and that Kenna didn't appear surprised by the less-than-welcoming gesture. "I'll go make sure Tina has dinner in order," Sutton continued. "Make yourself comfortable, Major. Kenna."

The air left the room as soon as they were alone. She was both too far away and too close for his peace of mind. Questions hovered on the tip of his tongue. Questions that she anticipated, based on her expectant—slightly defiant—expression. But the bag of rejected jerky she'd brought looked so sad, dangling against her boot. And he didn't like the welcome she'd received. Not at all. Knew it had to account for the steel she'd put in her spine, the adorable way she lifted her chin. So he didn't ask why she'd kept her identity from him. Yes, because he didn't want to be predictable, but more so because he wanted to distract her from the tense undercurrents he'd felt running through the room. He needed her to feel welcome, even if it wasn't his place or his home.

"I'm not much of a fan of dinner parties." He cleared his throat into the silence. "You ever hear of murder mystery dinner theater?" She shook her head slowly, as if trying to discern his angle. "There's a place down in Atlanta—Agatha's, I think it's called. From the time my sister and I entered middle school, my mother used to drag us there for our birthdays. These actors would put on a big whodunit on stage while everyone ate ribs."

A spark lit her eyes. "So bad it was good?"

"Exactly." *Oh God, she's so damn pretty and I'm stuck talking about dinner theater.* "We started off hating it every time, but then my mother, she'd start laughing. She'd laugh so loud, the actors would forget their lines. Soon none of us could keep a straight face." He shrugged. "I think that's why I can't enjoy dinner parties anymore. They pale in comparison."

"I hate be the bearer of bad news, True Blue, but this one is going to keep the disappointment streak alive."

"Now, see, you missed the point of the story." Beck sidestepped an ottoman and risked a move in her direction. "I was going to tell you that this dinner party already beat the others. Just from having you walk in."

The plastic bag of beef jerky hit the floor, spilling its contents. On reflex, Beck stooped down to pick it up, which was a grave mistake if he'd ever made one because it put him eye level with her thighs. He tangled a hand in the plastic bag so he wouldn't touch her. Ducked his head so he wouldn't look, either. Just a peek had been enough to dry his throat and make his dress pants feel three sizes too small.

He started to shove the packets of jerky back into the bag, but stilled when he felt Kenna's hand brush over his shaved head. "I told you, Major. You're allowed to look at my body."

"Not right now, I can't." His tone was harsh so he softened it. "Wouldn't be right in your father's house."

She hummed in a low, soothing way that made him close his eyes. "Not a lot of men would care."

"Those men aren't worthy of your time." He twisted the plastic in his fist. "Speaking of which, I'd like to know if you're spoken for, Kenna."

"No. I don't let men speak for me." A few beats of silence passed during which thick, consuming tension drained from Beck. "Why aren't you pissed at me?" she asked, her nails trailing down his neck and back up. "For not telling you who I was."

Her touch was torture and he never wanted her to stop. Ever. But he forced himself to move away before he lost the battle and looked at her legs. Maybe even let his hands encounter that supple skin. "I'm not pissed about that. I'm only curious why." Beck rose from his crouched position, watching her breath go shallow when he reached his full height. Did she *like* tall men? He hoped so. "I'm only angry that you left. Before I could…"

"Before you could what?" She moved closer, just close enough to graze his rib cage with her breasts and turn his cock to steel. "What would you have done to me, Major?"

*Breathe, man. In and out.* "I won't say the words under your father's roof."

She traced his belt buckle with a single finger. "But you would tell me outside?"

"Only if you'll give me the chance to do what I say."

Confusion and indecision flashed in her green eyes. "I assumed you would go out last night to celebrate being back. Finding a girl to pick up where I left off wouldn't have been hard." She swiped a palm against her skirt as she stepped back. "You didn't…do that?"

"I went out for a couple beers by myself." He hadn't wanted to, but the silent gray apartment had forced him out, just to encounter the noise to which he'd grown accustomed, back in the bustling Army facility he'd lived in so long. He should have gone to find Cullen, have the discussion he'd been putting off, but he'd wanted to give his friend one more night with a clear conscience. A luxury Beck didn't have. "There were girls there, yeah. Smiling and dancing. But I couldn't take my eyes off the door hoping you might walk in."

"Jesus," she breathed. "Stop saying things like that to me."

"Why?"

"I—you should save those pretty sentiments for someone who will appreciate them."

The flush on her cheeks told Beck she appreciated them just fine, but he wouldn't call her on it. Not just yet. She might get angry, and he had plans to kiss her this time around. "So you want me to detail how I'd like to touch you. You want me to look at your body, but you draw the line at me saying nice things."

"That about sums it up."

He scratched his jaw. "You've given me something to think on, Kenna."

Sutton swung open the kitchen door then, calling them to the table. Beck threw a wink at Kenna and gestured for her to precede him.

* * *

Kenna twirled a forkful of pasta and let it unwind. Her appetite had apparently gone on sabbatical. Or the floating lust balloons bumping around in her stomach simply left no room for food. Although battling the urge to climb across the table and straddle the major's lap was eminently wrong, considering her father sat three feet away, that's exactly what she wanted to do. Highly unlike her in so many ways. She'd been at dozens of these dinners with her father, honoring one soldier or another. Mostly it turned out to be an excuse for the lieutenant general to relate his own stories. And usually the guest sent a discreet glance or nine at her cleavage throughout the meal. A perfect amount to remind her men only wanted one thing, thus justifying her plans to remain unattached. It wasn't a cynical practice. Just a little reward for being practical. Seeing the male-female dynamic for what it was. A necessary function that rarely survived in the long term.

Beck hadn't glanced at her rack once. Not once. He was a giant, sexy, unassuming phenomenon, and she didn't like it. Upstairs in the old brain chamber, that is. The upstairs chamber that housed intelligent thought wanted to put him in a clean-cut category. One that made sense and didn't throw her ideas about men into a freaking tailspin. Downstairs, however? Downstairs liked his resolve very much. Couldn't wait to break through it when the timing was right. Shake him up again like she'd done yesterday.

Those were the two key parts of Kenna she was comfortable addressing. Upstairs and downstairs. The middle…the middle was off limits. That clumsy, clunking organ in her chest shouldn't have sped up when Beck said sweet words. It should have disregarded them as a line. A ploy to get into her pants and finally lose that pesky virginity. And she might have pulled it off if he would just stop smiling that half smile at her across the table and start looking at her boobs and not her eyes. What was wrong with him? This bra was a man *assassin*, pushing those puppies up in a way that usually had members of the opposite sex groaning when she passed. She might as well be wearing a hockey jersey for all the attention Beck paid them.

Oh, it was on. In more ways than one. As soon as they

were alone, she would snuff out this wayward blip on the radar screen and everything would make sense again. She'd slake her mega-watt—frankly, *embarrassing*—attraction for Beck tonight. He would head back to Georgia in a matter of days with his newfound knowledge of the female body and set to work using it right away, probably snatching up some chesty milkmaid or whatever the hell they had on tap down there. She'd be nothing but a fond memory to him and she could go back to meaningless, road trip hookups every few months.

Beck's gaze met hers, one dark blond eyebrow cocked as if she'd voiced the thought aloud. Could this man read her mind? Back in the living room, she'd gotten that sense. Best to remember he was apparently one of the Army's sharpest minds. Not *just* a peach farmer who not only remembered the manners he'd been taught, but stuck to them like Gorilla Glue.

"Are you sure you won't stay past Wednesday night's ceremony, Major Collier?"

The mind-reading major gave a reluctant head shake. "Much as I'd like to stay a while, sir, I need to be back in Georgia. My grandfather is getting on in years and needs help around the farm, harvesting the peaches and such."

Her father wiped the corners of his mouth. "I try to imagine a mind like yours going toward peach farming and I just can't. We need you training new recruits, here at Black Rock, passing on your problem-solving ability."

"All due respect, sir, I put in my time." His smile matched his good-natured tone. "I think you'd be surprised how much strategy goes into farming. My mind won't be wasted; I'll just be switching focus."

Kenna took a long sip of her Diet Coke, watching Beck over the rim of her glass. No matter how personal or unintentionally condescending her father's questions became, he kept his cool. Not a stutter or hesitation. He didn't have to think about his answers because he was telling the truth. Somehow she didn't have a single doubt of that. Not for the first time since they met, she wondered who would land this man. How easy it would be to trust him if a woman allowed herself.

During the course of the meal, she'd learned more about Beck's time overseas. His ability to find patterns and devise unique and often diplomatic ways to ended crises. He'd had the option of coming home more than once, but had turned it down. Although Beck had mentioned to her father that going home and leaving behind his fellow soldiers hadn't felt right, Kenna had a feeling it was more. While the major might be unassuming, she had a hunch Beck knew his talent made a difference. The kind between life and death.

"There's a ceremony coming up?" Kenna asked, surprising herself. She hadn't spoken since they'd sat down, unable to fit in a word edgewise around her father.

Beck looked uncomfortable for the first time that night. "There's a medal ceremony I've been asked to attend—"

"Asked to attend?" Her father interrupted with a rumbling laugh. "He's the honoree. Major Collier is being presented with a Silver Star."

"Oh," she whispered, wondering why he'd never mentioned it. Wasn't an impending honor something a soldier would be proud of? Why did he look so uneasy? "Congratulations, Major."

"Yes, congratulations," Tina echoed with a smile as she

rose from the table. Kenna stood to help her father's wife remove the empty plates, but the older woman gestured for her to sit back down. "More whiskey, gentlemen?"

Kenna noticed Beck frowning at her nearly empty Diet Coke. "No, ma'am," he said. "One was enough for me. It might be a short drive back to the barracks, but it's still driving."

Her father leaned back as Tina took away his plate and disappeared into the kitchen. "Have another, son. Kenna can drive you home. It's on her way to the garage."

While her pulse began pounding in her ears, Beck's frown only deepened. "Garage?"

"I live in an apartment above a garage on the south perimeter of base," she explained, before her father could jump in. "They let me use an empty warehouse downstairs for my work."

"What work is that?"

Had his voice gotten deeper? Kenna suddenly felt like they were the only two people in the room, everything else blurring into nothingness as he zeroed in on her. Held her still under his regard. Oh God, she was going to drive him home. Just the knowledge that they would share the enclosed space of her car once more made her thighs squeeze together. "I'm a welder. I create metal sculptures."

The right corner of his mouth lifted. "Yeah?"

Before she could answer, Tina stuck her head out from the kitchen. "Joseph—I mean, Lieutenant General—there is a call for you. Colonel Wheeler."

"I'll take it in the study." Her father slapped his chair's armrests and stood. Beck immediately followed his lead. "I'm afraid this man is as long-winded as they come." He nodded at Kenna. "It could be a while, so I won't keep you sitting here. Both of you get home safe."

Beck saluted her father and the older man followed suit before leaving the room.

Then they were alone again. The table seemed to shrink between them, as if tempting her to do as she craved—crawl across it and launch herself at Beck. He'd managed to hide every trace of desire for her during dinner, but how would he fare if they touched?

His easygoing demeanor had departed the room with her father. His cheekbones appeared more pronounced and tinged with red, his hands curled into fists.

"Ready to go?" she asked, inwardly cringing at the breathless quality of her voice.

"No."

"No?"

His eyes cut to the side, then back. "If I stand up, you're going to see what happens when you look at me that way for over an hour, Kenna."

"What way is that?"

She could tell he was struggling not to look at her cleavage. Inside, she was begging him to, but his gaze remained locked on hers. "Like maybe you're planning on doing something bad."

Kenna could hear Tina washing dishes in the kitchen and knew from experience the woman wouldn't seek Kenna out or re-enter the room. Working as a tech specialist, Tina had lived on base during Kenna's wild streak and didn't seem prepared to forget about it any time soon. She couldn't be more grateful for the woman's aversion to her now, though, because cracking Beck's determination had just become a challenge she couldn't refuse. He was an immovable rock staring her down from across the table, but she saw more. She saw desperation, pain and hunger—all for her—and she needed to be the one thing that could shake him. Save him. Just for tonight, she wanted to be someone's requirement to go on breathing.

When she rose from the table, he interpreted her expression right away, shaking his head. "What are you doing?"

Without answering, she circled the table and trailed a finger across the massive breadth of his powerful shoulders. They began rising and falling, seeming to expand with each movement. It reminded her of his size, as if additional thoughts were necessary. His obvious strength was the turn-on because it was kept so tightly leashed. She wanted to snap that leash.

Whether or not he'd done it consciously, Beck had leaned back into her touch, leaving a gap of room between his body and the table. Kenna stepped into that space now, between his parted legs, and ran her hands up his muscled chest. Beck's head fell back on a rough exhale. "Kenna, I've got a strong will, but you're testing the hell out of it." The column of his throat worked. "This isn't right. Not here."

She looked down and saw the thick ridge of his erection, outlined where it lay against his belly. Anticipation sent dampness spreading between her legs. *Need him inside me. Need him to need me back*. "When you think about your first time, Major…" She flicked open the top two buttons of her shirt. "Am I on top, riding your big body? Or do you have me on my back, taking it hard?"

His tight-lipped groan sent a shiver pulsing up her

thighs. "Don't make me say these things here. I'm trying to do this right."

Trying to do *what* right? Be respectful to her father... or something else? She didn't want to know, so she finished opening the trail of buttons and parted the thin material of her shirt. He managed to keep his gaze plastered to the ceiling until she unsnapped the front clasp of her bra. His head came up, eyes blazing as her bare breasts bounced free. "*Jesus Christ*." His tongue dragged along his bottom lip like a man getting ready for a meal, but instead of feasting on her, he said, "I could live off the sight of you, darlin'. But if you don't put your shirt back on, I'll hold you down and do it myself."

Her sex clenched at his words, the mental image of Beck angrily dressing her. "I'll put my shirt back on if you answer my question."

Kenna stepped closer, bringing her breasts within an inch of his mouth, and his entire body shuddered. "What was the question again?"

"Your first time." His puffs of breath made her nipples tighten. "Me on top? Or you?"

For a split second, she thought he might give in and suck one of her peaks into his mouth, but he remained in place. "When I first saw you, I thought of..."

"Tell me, Major," she whispered hoarsely. "Say all the bad things in your head."

His swallow was audible. "I wanted to hold you down and—and fuck you. Without holding back. I wanted to push your legs wide open and fuck you while your nails made my back bleed." The words were rushed, out of breath. "Even if you screamed, I didn't want to stop. Just wanted to pump and fuck until I stopped thinking and only felt you." His hands shot out to grip the sides of her open shirt, closing the material over her breasts with a heavy, relieved exhale. "But I'd want you on top, Kenna. I don't think we could do it the other way. Wouldn't I hurt you, darlin'? You're so small compared to me."

Very few times in her life had Kenna been struck speechless. Beck's graphic description of what he wanted to do with her blazed through her middle like a lightning storm, but the sweetness that followed, his covering her breasts, laid a balm over the scorched earth left behind. She felt pulled in two directions and each one was equally appealing. Sex with him wouldn't be as black and white as she'd hoped. The tingling in her neck said *run, run away and don't look back*, but when she remained silent too long and a hint of vulnerability crept into his expression, she knew it would never happen.

Messy or not, she was running headfirst into the oncoming storm.

# CHAPTER FIVE

Beck studied Kenna from the passenger seat, wishing like hell she'd say something.

See? This is why he kept his sinful thoughts to himself. Since Beck could remember, he'd been tested by desires that a good man had no right to feel. At age fourteen, he'd even gotten the nerve up to confide in the youth minister at his church, but instead of giving Beck a way to control the urges, he'd been instructed to ignore the need to…rut. Not just to have sex, but to recreate the sweaty, flesh-slapping images his mind conjured up. He'd been told that they were the work of the devil, that lovemaking was a quiet, caring act shared between husband and wife. Over time, he'd learned to keep the thoughts at bay until late at night, in the dark, when they wouldn't remain caged any longer. It had worked well enough until Kenna had sauntered up to him at the landing zone and mental hell had broken loose.

Everything he'd said to her had been truthful. The afternoon he'd woken up to find her gone, he'd been so painfully erect, he'd been forced to ease himself before rising from the bed had been an option. She'd poked the sleeping bear inside him and now it roared through his insides, looking for its mate. Last night in the bar, he'd only been capable of mustering a mild appreciation for other women, much like he'd felt for the female soldiers he'd encountered overseas. But he'd *needed* Kenna. Only Kenna. Didn't even want to consider someone else's hands on him. Or *hers* on someone else.

Beck had to close his eyes and count to ten, surprised once again by the depth of jealousy the thought of her with someone else incurred. He was leaving Thursday morning, the day after the ceremony. Leaving for good. There wasn't a man alive with the power of sight who wouldn't want her for himself. On top of being every male's sexual fantasy on two legs, she had a quick sense of humor. She was *interesting*. Intelligent. Mysterious. Knowing how quickly she'd be spoken for, he could already tell boarding that plane on Thursday would be like getting caught in a tunnel blast a second time. Worse.

His dark realization was cut short when Kenna pulled up outside a greasy, dilapidated garage. "Tell me you don't live here. Please."

"Afraid so, Major." She cut off the car's engine. "Still want to come inside, or have you changed your mind?"

"I have not changed my mind." Great. Finally, he gets her talking only to insult her home. "I beg your pardon, Kenna. I didn't mean to come off rude."

A smile entered her eyes. "You're begging my pardon?"

"Yes, ma'am." He looked back toward the garage, noticing the sign advertising break inspections was seconds from plummeting to the ground. "It just doesn't seem safe for a girl living alone, is all. Doesn't your father object?"

"I'm an adult, Major. I decide where to lay my head." She shrugged. "Besides, I think as long as I moved out and gave Tina room to move in, I could have gone to the moon for all he cared."

Beck experienced the same irritation he felt when the lieutenant general hadn't thanked her for the beef jerky, and then again when Tina hadn't offered her a drink. "I don't like you being treated that way."

She stared through the windshield for a moment before returning her attention to him. Gone was the forlorn quality in her expression. Invitation had taken its place. "You know, talking about this doesn't put me in a sexy mood." She unbuckled her seatbelt and leaned across the console, casting a net of her incense scent to drag him under. Her hand landed on his thigh, but it might as well have been his cock from the way it immediately strained against his fly. "I want to hear more about what you want. What you told me back at the house…I liked it, Major. A lot."

"You ought to start calling me Beck, now, Kenna." Lord, her breasts swelled against her shirt as she leaned toward him. "Seeing as how you're taking me home."

Her hand skated higher on his thigh. "Okay…Beck."

That was it. Kenna saying his name blew a fuse in his head, short-circuiting his self-control. A *boomboomboom* started in his ears as he yanked her across the console, dropping her firm, little backside onto his lap. Every second of resistance he'd managed back in that dining room demanded repayment and nothing could settle the debt, save her. Before he knew his own mind, he ripped her shirt open and upclasped her bra, growling as those rosy-peaked, bad-girl tits popped free. "I'm going to suck them. *Need* to suck them." He bent his head and dragged her right nipple into his mouth, drawing on it with a loud moan. "Move around on my dick while I suck you, Kenna. I'm so hard. You make me so hard to be inside you. How is that possible when I don't even know what it feels like?"

She turned in his lap to straddle him, one palm smoothing down the side of his face. "Take me upstairs and I'll show you." Her breathing was erratic, but she stopped after one mind-bending buck of her hips. "Don't you know you make me just as achy?"

Awe and relief and *lust* battered him. "I want to see that spot where you're achy. I want to look at you there, watch you touch it. I want to touch…your pussy. Want to lick it."

Kenna fell forward onto his chest, forehead dropping onto his shoulder. "Beck, if you keep talking like that, I'm going to come before you get inside me."

"I don't think I want that to happen." With an iron will she continued to diminish with every hot breath against his neck, Beck pushed open the passenger door and stepped out, smiling through the pleasure-pain of Kenna clinging to him like a lifeline. Ah hell, he liked that. Like her compact body wrapped around his like a missing piece, her curves accommodating his ridges, the valley between her legs, warm and inviting, settling on top of his throbbing dick. "Tell me where I'm going, darlin'," he choked out.

She ran her open mouth up his neck. "There's an alley on the left…staircase around back."

Beck strode toward the alley, unable to ignore how poorly lit and deserted it was. Anger and worry trickled through the permanent heat she'd inflicted on him. "I don't like this. I don't like you here." She tugged on his ear with her teeth and his stride faltered. *Distracting me. It's working. For now.* He stomped up the staircase, groaning at the way she slid up and down his bulging fly with each step. "While we're on the subject of things I don't like, Kenna, I haven't even kissed your mouth. You can be damn sure that'll be happening before we go any further—"

Her mouth landed on his just as they reached the door. Sweet Lord above. If he'd thought Kenna simply walking into a room had an impact on him, he'd had another think coming. His back hit her front door, air seeping from his lungs as she locked their mouths together and slowly dragged away, taking his bottom lip with her. Both of their mouths opened on cue for a pull of oxygen before melding together, meshing hotly, moving in a slow, sexual rhythm, matched by the pulsing between his thighs. As if she'd made an unexpected discovery, she climbed higher on his body, thighs gripping his sides, hands holding his head steady as she delivered the kiss of his life. As soon as the notion rocked through his fevered brain, he reversed their positions, shoving her up against the door, determined to deliver the same to her. Their tongues tangled in an eager slide and he finally let himself do what he'd been fantasizing about since yesterday. He reached beneath her skirt and manhandled her sinner's backside. He gripped the taut flesh and tightened his hold, lifting and stroking. She alleviated any fear he had of being too rough by moaning into his mouth, digging her heels into his waist.

Kenna tore her mouth away. "Inside, Beck. Take me inside," she wheezed. "If I didn't know any better, I'd think you'd done this before. A lot."

"Nah, darlin'. Just you." He took the single key she offered, turning it in the lock. "You make everything I do feel right. That has nothing to do with experience." Walking them into the darkened apartment, he kissed her collarbone. "Thinking maybe that's all to do with Kenna."

Her legs dropped from around his waist. She turned before he could see her expression, but he knew he'd said too much. Shown his hand too early. When the light came on, there was a line of tension in her shoulders. *No.* He wouldn't let her shut him out after they'd come this far. Hadn't she said he made her ache, too? When she'd taken off her bra, he'd never been more turned on in his life. Would it work in reverse? Figuring he had nothing—except everything—to lose, Beck started unbuttoning his dress shirt. When he'd nearly reached the bottom, Kenna turned, shifting in her boots. Her green gaze sparked like a firecracker when he tugged the hem from his waistband. "W-what are you—"

Right before Beck let his shirt drop, he remembered the wound in his side and lifted a hand to hide it. Jesus, if this girl could make him forget the painful shrapnel wound, she could do anything. But he'd never willingly shown it to anyone, and he didn't want her pity. He wanted her to need him. Needed her lust. Her touch. Anything but pity.

Kenna came to him, tension still visible in her shoulders, but it was a different kind. "I thought you were in a support unit." Her hand hovered over the wound, as if trying to cure it. "You saw action, too?"

"I did. Of course I did." He ran a thumb over her top lip, relieved to see her eyelids flutter. "I wouldn't send men into a situation where I wouldn't go myself."

She traced the edge of his wound with her finger. "You're a good man, Beck Collier. Some woman is going to snatch you up one day and never let go."

Something akin to denial speared his chest and spiked his temper. He tipped her chin up and stooped down to bring their faces close. "Don't talk about me with some other woman when I came here to be inside *your* body, Kenna. Because I promise you this." He backed her toward the living room. "I aim to get so deep inside you, neither one of us will think of *anyone* else for a damn long while." *Ever again,* if he had his way. "Now get your clothes off and show me the only woman I have plans to fuck. Show me."

A beat passed in the living room where Beck thought he'd gone too far. Showed too early the secret, primitive part of himself he'd worked to suppress. Let more honesty slip out than was acceptable. It all vanished into the racing river of his pulse when she smiled, slow and sensual. "You know, I thought you were all sugar when we met." She let her tattered shirt slide to the floor, palmed her breasts in a way that nearly brought him to his knees. "But you're just a little bad underneath the sweet exterior, aren't you?" She swayed toward him, right into his space. He thought she might kiss him, but she nudged him backward instead, sending him down into a deep-bottomed leather arm chair. "Why don't we find out exactly how deep the bad goes, Major?"

* * *

Out of self-preservation, Kenna pretended not to see the absolute possession in Beck's eyes as she removed her bra and kicked off her boots. If she let herself think about the hints he'd been dropping, her intuition that he wanted more than a one-night stand, her conscience wouldn't allow her to go through with it. Unfortunately, her body gave her zero choice in the matter. She'd known Beck was a large man, a *handsome* man, but then he'd gone and taken off his shirt. If she stared at his brick-house body any harder, she'd need smelling salts to be revived. The angry wound in his side, the jagged, rough-hewn cut of his muscles made him rugged when she'd been expecting a teddy bear. Uh-uh. Not Beck. Beck was ripped as shit, and that little display of anger he'd let slip through the cracks had made him unexpectedly dangerous. He was a coin with two very appealing sides and she wanted to flip him, see where he landed. Since danger suited her need to keep this temporary fling as casual as possible, she would be anything but sweet. Memorable? Hell yes. But not sweet.

When only her short black skirt remained, she used Beck's shoulders for balance. She placed her knees on opposite arms of the chair, leaving her center exposed for his perusal, shielded only by a sheer red pair of panties. Beck cursed under his breath, the muscles of his chest and abdomen shifting powerfully, making her even bolder. She took a moment to tease the hem of her skirt before sliding the material over her hips, baring the wispy red thong that barely covered her center. "You want to touch me where I ache, Beck?" She nudged aside the red strip with two fingers, whimpering as they made contact with her sensitive clitoris. Her eyes tried to close at the flood of pleasure when she circled her nub once and pressed down, but she kept them open. On Beck. "Right here, sweetheart?"

"*Yes*. Christ, yes."

She slid her hands up to cup her breasts and squeezed, thigh muscles tightening at the delicious quickening in her belly. "I'm all yours."

Beck shot forward, latching his mouth to her clit, sucking her panties and flesh into his mouth on a thunderous growl. Kenna screamed at the unexpected action, nearly losing her balance until his hands molded to her bottom, holding her steady as he sucked. *Licked.* Oh God. Her body convulsed, stuttering just on the edge of orgasm. Impossible. Too soon. Wasn't it?

He pulled back by the barest of inches, his rapid puffs of breath feathering over her flesh. "D-do you like this?"

"*Yeskeepgoing.*"

"Thank *God.* Tastes so good."

Beck made contact again and Kenna's mind shut down, focusing only on the perfection of his suctioning mouth. He was a starved man who'd forgotten his last meal and needed sustenance. One of his brawny arms wrapped around her hips, freeing his other hand to slip between her thighs, a thumb brushing her entrance. As if he wanted her permission but refused to stop tonguing her damp core long enough to ask.

"Yours, Beck. My body is yours." Words she'd never said to anyone, would probably never say again. *Don't think about it. Focus on him…what he's doing to you.* "Touch me, move me, enter me, speak to me however it feels right. Everything you do will be *right.*"

She could feel something give way inside his big body. If possible, his mouth worked her harder, opening wide to draw on her flesh, then bathing her clit with his tongue. Two long fingers filled her and she gasped—*yes*—making eye contact with Beck as he broke away with a groan. "Ah, Kenna." His voice was a bed of nails. "I'm going to hurt you. I never knew…I didn't know you'd be so small." He wrapped his arms around her waist, buried his face against her stomach. "I take back what I said. I don't want to make you scream. Don't want you in pain."

Her throat constricted so hard she couldn't draw air for a moment, but Beck's obvious physical torment snapped her into action. She lifted his face to meet hers. "Unfasten your pants, Major. You won't hurt me." Their lips brushed. "If it hurts a little, the good will outweigh it. Okay?" She kissed him long and deep. "I showed you my ache, now show me yours."

His hands fell to his lap, bringing the sounds of leather sliding, his zipper descending. "If I do something to hurt you…" He broke off, shaking his head.

"Hey." As soon as his erection was free between them, large and beautiful, she pushed him against the chair back. "You're the virgin. That's supposed to be my line."

An intense glow lit his eyes. "You're in deep with me, Kenna Sutton."

"I know," she whispered, hiding her shaken reaction to his vow by reaching for the unopened pack of condoms in her side table, but her trembling fingers gave her away.

Beck took the box and ripped it open with his teeth, effectively replacing her embarrassment with another whopping dose of heat. He took out a foil wrapper, tore it on one end and rolled the condom down his erection. "I know this much from health class," he explained with a lopsided smile.

Something pointy stuck in her throat, but she swallowed

it with resolution. Thighs still spread wide, knees resting on opposite armrests, she took him in her hand, led him between her thighs and sank down, inch by inch. Beck gritted out her name at the ceiling, his neck and arm muscles constricting. Kenna's thighs felt the strain of her position, but she refused to change it because—*damn damn damn*—he couldn't possibly get any deeper. So huge and thick and smooth. Amazing. He pressed against her inner walls, stretching her to fit him and it hurt, but the hurt was glorious. Nothing compared to this. Nothing. The need to move was fast becoming an undeniable yen, so she dug her fingers into the leather back of the chair and rose, before dropping down onto him once again.

"*Oh my God.*"

"You? Christ. Oh, Christ. You have no idea..." He lifted his hips, bringing them both off the seat. "It's too good. You're tight. So fucking tight and I can't. You can't move like that. Do it again. Okay, darlin'? Again. *Again.*"

She'd never wanted to kiss a man during sex, but hell if she didn't want to make out with his flushed, masculine face, the promise of a too-soon, blistering climax be damned. *Beck.* Sweet, sexual beast that had been pacing his cage too long. Kenna twisted her hips and pleasure spread like spilled ink in her middle. Never mind about the kissing. She'd only had this man inside her for thirty seconds and her body was sprinting blindly toward relief, lip-lock be damned. Kenna lifted and came down on him with a quick flick of her hips, moaning as Beck grew even larger inside her.

"I'm not leaving you in need again." Beck thrust up into her with a strangled groan. "But I can't think when you're doing that. Can't think about anything 'cept coming inside your body."

"Don't think, Beck. I don't want you to think." Reminding herself this was his first experience, Kenna took his hands and placed them on her backside, her breath leaving in a rush when he gripped her with punishing strength. "Move me how you want me, Beck. Grind me down, bounce me, make me ride you slow. Do whatever makes you come the hardest."

Sweat had broken out along his upper lip, his sexy, corded neck. "I already know you're going to be the best of my life, Kenna. How do I make sure I'm the best of yours? *Tell me*."

*There's no one in the world like this guy.* "I like it hard." Her voice wavered. "Slam me down. Use my body to jack yourself off."

His eyes closed briefly before they opened and scorched a path over her breasts, belly, thighs. "You can't be real. You can't be."

Even though she'd instructed him, Kenna wasn't prepared for what followed. With the flesh of her bottom clenched in his hands, he impaled her on his unforgiving hardness, again and again. It started at a testing pace but grew almost out of control. Her teeth rattled inside her mouth with each life-affirming impact. Beck watched her through eyes at half-mast, eyes that glittered with so much pent-up lust, it staggered her. He tilted his hips, satisfaction conquering his expression when she moaned loud enough to shake the windows. Unbelievable. He was searching for her pleasure when this should have been about him. His first time. With the unimaginable sensations blasting her, she couldn't find the same selflessness. No, she'd never needed relief so badly.

She held her fingers over Beck's mouth. "Lick them." When he did as she asked, his tongue stroking her fingertips like their taste was incomparable, Kenna almost climaxed then and there. No more waiting. As Beck continued to slam her down on his erection, Kenna found her clit and with two rough circles of her middle finger, she pushed over into oblivion. "Yes, yes, *yes.*" *Oh holy shit*, her legs spasmed violently on the armrests, moisture flooding over the spot her body joined with Beck's. "So good, Beck. You're so *good.*"

A surprised whimper escaped her lips as he rose from the chair and flipped her over. No sooner had her back met the leather seat than her legs were secured over Beck's shoulders. A savage drive of his length into her still-contracting core stole a scream from her throat.

"Beck!"

Anguish infiltrated the sexual urgency on his face. "Am I hurting you?"

"N-*no.* Keep going, *keep going.*"

Wet flesh slapped together as he gripped her ankles where they rested on either side of his head and thrust. Thrust so hard Kenna knew she'd feel it for a week. "Scream, then," he growled in her ear, hips starting to pump at a brutal pace. "If it doesn't hurt, then scream."

She had no choice as another orgasm shuddered through her middle at Beck's unexpected aggression. More, more. She couldn't get enough. Wanted to be *made* to take everything he had to give. "That's right," she breathed, barely able to hear herself over the roaring pulse in her ears. "No holding back. Take out the frustration on me. In me."

"*Jesus. Stop*, Kenna." His fingers dug into her ankles. "I don't want this to end, but you're making it *so damn hard.*"

She responded with words even she couldn't comprehend. Again. He was going to make her come *again*, and she simultaneously wanted no part of it while needing it more than life itself.

"You like it hard, darlin'? I should have known." She clenched around him, and he gritted his teeth around a groan. "Leading me around by the cock with your sinner's body. Taking your tits out when I can't suck them. *Bad* girl." He bore down, grinding their joined bodies together. "Use your body to jack myself off? What do you think I'll be doing every time I touch myself for the rest of my fucking life? Thinking about you with your legs spread, asking to see my aching dick. Thinking about what those little red panties cover."

He drove home his point by ripping the half-shredded thong from her body, tossing it aside. Kenna couldn't see or think or process anything but the raging pleasure drowning her. She dug her nails into his pumping ass—*hard*—feeling the skin break and merely digging deeper. Her body tightened and twisted, overcome by a tumult of lust so strong she couldn't breathe. It poured through her shaking limbs, gathered in her belly and broke free.

Beck filled what little vision she had, head thrown back as he rammed himself deep one last time and went flying right along with her. "Oh, *Christ*. Kenna. *Kenna*." The sight of such a robust giant of a man trembling imprinted itself on her brain, never to fade. Neither would the weight of him as he fell forward, gathering her close and whispering in her ear, out of breath. "So beautiful. You know you're so beautiful and sweet, right, Kenna? I didn't mean those bad things I said. I just—"

Heart thudding double time in her chest, she covered his mouth with one hand. "Nothing we do or say together is wrong." When his furrowed brow began to ease in degrees, she removed her hand. "You were amazing, True Blue. That's kind of an epic understatement, actually, but my brain has left the building."

When color flared in his cheekbones, something shifted inside Kenna. Something sharp and boulder-sized. It alarmed her so much, she jolted beneath Beck's huge frame. Before she could scramble away, he scooped her up in his arms and stood. Without instructing him where her bedroom was located, he found it on the first try, nudging the door open with his foot. He didn't bother turning on the light, but laid her down with exaggerated gentleness in the center of her queen-sized bed, which was laughable since he'd just full-on screwed her brains out. But she couldn't manage a laugh around the panic when he climbed into bed with her.

"Y-you're staying?"

"Yes, ma'am." She couldn't see his face in the darkness, but his breath feathered over her lips. "And I wouldn't advise asking me to leave when I'm feeling this way."

Her heart rioted. *Thud thud thud.* "Which way is that?"

"Like I've laid claim to what's mine. And I need to—to guard her now." A beat of silence vanished into the darkness. "I can't put it any more plainly, Kenna."

As her mind reeled, Beck drew her up against his chest, brawny arms wrapping around her body, one hand cradling her head. Oh God. Her first sleepover…and it felt permanent.

But nothing was permanent. This, especially, couldn't be permanent. Just as soon as she caught a few minutes of sleep, she'd figure out how to shake the guy.

Drowsiness coupled with Beck's warmth dragged her down, making resistance futile.

Just a few minutes.

She was asleep ten seconds later.

# CHAPTER SIX

Beck woke to the smell of incense and buried his face closer to the source. No. They were sheets, not Kenna. It smelled better on her skin, and he wanted to get a fix. Where was she? Beck cracked an eye open in the early morning light and searched for her across the bed. Not there. He sat up too quickly, causing his head to swim, but it gave him the second he needed to calm himself. They were in her apartment, after all. She couldn't have gone too far. Even if the apartment was so silent and still he could hear his own sprinting heartbeat.

He untangled himself from the flannel sheets and stood, marveling how rested he felt. Lord, he'd slept like the dead after what they'd done. Had she been expecting him to wake up last night for round two? He wrapped a hand around his heavy cock and groaned. Round two was a definite possibility right now, but a nagging intuition told him Kenna would still be in bed if that's what she wanted. Would he ever face another day without wanting what she'd given him last night? He doubted it. Doubted he'd want it with anyone else, either.

He'd always figured his first time would be a necessary evil, a jumping off point after which he'd get better. Learn how to please a woman. But Kenna, she'd been pleased. More than that, she'd given him a glimpse at her vulnerability. He hadn't expected that, and the woman beneath had addicted him more than sex ever could. If she was still lying in bed, Beck worried he might have crawled on top of her and demanded to know every single thought in her head. So maybe it was a good thing he'd been given this time alone to think before going to find her.

Beck pulled a throw blanket off the end of Kenna's bed and wrapped it around his waist. Unable to resist a quick look at her possessions, in the hopes it might give him some insight, he stopped in front of a framed picture on her dresser. A teenage Kenna in an oversized orange jumpsuit picking up garbage on the side of the road. She looked directly into the camera, her expression defiant. Daring the person snapping the photograph to comment. He recognized that look.

Growing up, his grandfather had owned a stable of horses, located just on the edge of the peach orchard. He didn't make a trade breeding, merely keeping them for pleasure riding and traversing the narrow orchard lanes. One afternoon, his grandfather had come home with a beautiful unbroken filly whose previous owners hadn't even succeeded in saddling her. Beck could remember the wariness in her brown eyes, the way she'd reared back when anyone got too close. *Stay away or else.* At least, that's what Beck's childhood imagination had interpreted from the filly's wild look. About a week passed of his grandfather approaching the horse with a bridle with no success. Then one of the mares had gone into labor—a difficult one. Shocking everyone, including the vet, the usually standoffish filly had stood outside the mare's stall throughout the night, refusing to budge.

Yeah. Beck had a fair idea that Kenna wouldn't take kindly to being compared to a horse, gorgeous as the filly had been or not. Be that as it may, he'd seen two sides of Kenna during the last couple days, whether or not she'd intended him to. Wild, wary Kenna and selfless, nurturing Kenna. The girl who'd flashed him in her father's house and the girl who'd been outraged at his lack of a welcome home. The girl who'd traced his shrapnel wound like she was willing him to heal.

Beck ran his thumb over the picture of Kenna stuffing garbage into a trash bag, wondering why she'd chosen to display this particular memory instead of a happy one. Did she have any happy ones? She better. He wouldn't appreciate knowing she'd been unhappy.

With one last glance at the picture, he left Kenna's bedroom, already knowing he wouldn't find her in the apartment. He tried unsuccessfully not to stare at the armchair where she'd blown his mind hours before. The way he'd spoken to Kenna hadn't horrified her at all. On the contrary. What else about his tastes could he reveal without turning her off? Resolving to think about it later, he quickly dressed in the living room. He patted his back pocket to make sure he had his wallet, frowning when he didn't find it. There. On the floor. Beck stooped down to pick it up, wincing when he saw it was open. A photograph taken at his high school's homecoming dance stared back at him. In it, he had his arms around Mary. Had Kenna seen this? If she was already spooked by them spending the night together, the picture definitely wouldn't help his cause.

The few words she'd spoken at dinner the night before were the only thing standing between him and alarm. *Workspace.* He remembered she mentioned that she had a workspace downstairs in the garage. On his way down the back stairs, he saw a flare of sparks through a plastic garage window. Heard a sound that called to mind harsh rain pinging off metal.

She didn't turn around when he walked through the open door. A good thing because the sight of her in frayed jean shorts, sexy lower back exposed, wielding a torch was just about the hottest thing he'd borne witness to in his twenty-six years. If her stiff shoulders and anxious energy weren't telling him loud and clear she wouldn't be receptive to touch, he'd already be working the button of her shorts, begging in her ear to let him give her an orgasm. His new favorite pastime.

Beck gave her wide berth as he circled the worktable, avoiding the blue sparks vanishing as they hit the concrete floor. She wore a mask, so it took an extra second for her to spot him in her peripheral vision. When she did, the sparks ceased immediately and the mask was pushed back onto her head.

"Morning," she said, with an impatient swipe at her face.

Avoiding his eyes, huh? Okay. Might have been expected, but it still made something spiky stick in his stomach. "Morning, Kenna." He started to ask her how she'd slept but a metal sculpture to his left, shining in a patch of sunlight, grabbed his attention. It stood nearly as tall as him and resembled a tree. The trunk had been fashioned from what looked like a car bumper whose edges had been rounded, reshaped to zigzag side to side. Pieces of metal in various shapes were attached at intervals, making him think of palm fronds. They'd each been painted a different vibrant color, and broken glass shards had been fashioned to the edges. Each component of the sculpture was striking on its own, but all together, the effect was extraordinary. "This is one of yours?"

A shuffle of boots behind him. "Yeah. It's mine."

He walked closer, seeing subtle nuances as he went. "Where do you get the parts?"

"Here at the garage, mostly. Scrap metal or discarded car parts." He turned to find her staring at him, but she quickly averted her gaze and began straightening tools on the worktable. "It's part of the reason I chose this place. Easy access to materials."

"Did you explain that to your father?"

"No." Her surprise at his question was clear. "He didn't ask."

Beck approached the bench, much the way his grandfather approached the filly all those years ago. She seemed to be bracing herself to run if he tried to reach out for her. And damn if he didn't want to touch her so bad his palms itched. *Keep her talking while you figure out how to get the privilege again.* "Why do you enjoy doing this?"

Her gaze snapped back to his. "What do you mean?"

"I want to know why you love it."

"I never said I loved it."

"Kenna, no one makes anything that beautiful unless they loved every minute of the process."

A hand flew to her mask, as if she was considering

flipping it back down to cover her face, but it dropped to her side after a beat. "Thank you. I do love it," she mumbled. "I guess I don't think pieces should be tossed in the trash because they have a dent. Or they're not perfect like the shiny new parts. They still have a use if you take some time to look."

*I am looking.* The words brushed the insides of his throat, seeking escape, but he swallowed them. They burned going down. Standing so close to her without speaking his mind got harder by the minute. It wasn't him. He might have an iron will when it came to most things, but apparently it didn't extend to her. There was a sense of urgency gaining strength, too. Leaving in two days. He was leaving in two days. Something needed to happen here and while he didn't know what just yet, a wind pressed at his back, telling him forward was the only acceptable direction.

"I'm seeing you again, Kenna Sutton. Don't try and pretend different."

Her mouth fell open. "Pretty confident for a one-timer, aren't you?"

Beck ground his teeth together, commanding himself to be patient. "Respectfully, darlin', it might have only been once for me, but if I counted correctly, it was three times for you."

A grin started to transform her mouth, but she banished it. "Look, Major—"

"I've slept in your sheets and seen my sweat cooling on your gorgeous skin. I've spent myself in your mouth and between your legs." Attempting to reel back his irritation, he very carefully placed his hands palm down on the table separating them. "You'll call me Beck."

"Beck, then," Kenna said, voice hoarse. She snatched up the torch, as if she had a mind to use it on him. "It's natural to get attached to the person you're with the first time. I certainly didn't, but I've heard that." Her smile was tight. "It'll fade, I swear."

*Patience, do not desert me now.* Every instinct screamed at him to drag her across the table, remind her of how deep their attraction ran, but he knew it would be a mistake. It would give her a reason to keep him away. "How long until it fades, you reckon?"

Kenna shrugged. "Probably when you go home and meet another big-haired, big-busted blonde. *Probably.*" She dropped her torch as if it were on fire. "*God.* I don't know why I said that."

All right. Safe to say she'd seen the photo in his wallet. "Kenna, I didn't keep that picture because I still have feelings for Mary." He sighed when she picked up a pencil and started to sketch on an oversized notepad. *Scratch. Scratch.* "It's a fond memory, a simple one. I needed as many as I could get over there. Didn't feel right throwing it away, even after what she did."

"We had one night together, Beck. No big deal. I don't know why you're even explaining this to me." She shoved the pencil behind her ear and fidgeted. "You don't see me going into detail about all my past boyfriends."

He saw it coming. Saw she'd located the weapon in her arsenal and was prepared to use it. "Don't—"

"You're not the first soldier I've brought back here from base, Beck. Far from it." She wouldn't look at him. Good thing, because in two sentences she'd managed to invoke jealousy and resignation he was *nowhere* near ready to feel.

Not because her having partners before him made him *want* her any less. No, he'd just hoped she wouldn't try to distance him with that knowledge. And like any man who felt for a woman, thinking of her with other men didn't sit well. At. All.

"So, what you're telling me is I'm a notch in your bedpost." His jaw was bunched so tight it hurt to speak. "I just want to be clear."

Her hesitation was brief. Too brief. But at least it told him he'd live to fight another day. "That about sums it up, *Beck*."

Not trusting himself to speak, he nodded once. It took every ounce of his will not to look back as he walked out the door. Back to his empty apartment on base.

He'd give her until tonight. No longer.

# CHAPTER SEVEN

Kenna stared out at the milling patrons of Bombs Away, her drink gone warm in her hand. The bar was packed tonight thanks to the live country western band currently playing "Sweet Home Alabama." For the third time. The crowd consisted almost entirely of Black Rock soldiers, most of them men, which made Kenna and Darla veritable celebrities. Neither of them were feeling very chatty, however, and their expressions must have mirrored that, because after two rounds of drinks had been sent their way and rejected, they'd been left alone. Alone. Just the way she liked it.

She took a hefty swallow of room-temperature bourbon, hoping it would douse the guilt and anxiousness burning in her stomach. It only kindled the fire. God, she felt like pond scum.

"Why do we come here?" Darla grumbled beside her. "They don't even have Wi-Fi."

"They have cheap liquor."

"Oh, right."

Kenna twisted a red cocktail straw around her middle finger, the movement restless. She didn't want to be at Bombs Away tonight any more than Darla, but avoidance had always been her knee-jerk reaction to anything uncomfortable, so why switch it up? If she stayed at her apartment, Beck might come over. And although she'd done her damnedest to sever their connection, if he showed up, she would drag him inside and ride him like a mountain bike. The best sex of her life just *had* to be with a stand-up guy, right? He just *had* to hold her so tightly while she slept that she woke with her heart lodged in her throat. At the very least, he could have been dismissive or ambivalent toward her work, right? No. No, he couldn't. Major Beck motherfucking Collier.

Darla batted the straw out of her hand. "Stop fidgeting. That's my thing."

"Ouch." She scowled at her friend. "What's *my* thing then?"

"Brooding. You're nailing it, by the way." Darla heaved a sigh and returned her attention to the crowd. "You know, this is a big enough sausage festival even *I* could get laid. Your impression of a gargoyle is foiling any chance I have of male interaction."

Kenna massaged her forehead. "I'm sorry. I dragged you out on a school night and I'm being a twat."

"Yes, you are, but I know how you can atone."

She quirked an eyebrow. *Go on.*

Darla dipped a finger into her cranberry juice and popped it into her mouth. "Tell me what happened with the virgin."

"What?" Her spine snapped straight. "Don't call him that. What?"

Darla snorted. "Your reaction is not telling whatsoever." She shifted in the cracked leather booth to face Kenna. "Come on. Unburden yourself. It'll be like, I don't know, losing your virginity or something."

"*You're* the twat."

"I'll own that." Darla stacked her hands beneath her chin and stared. "Wait-ing."

Kenna set her bourbon down with a *thunk*. "He…spent the night."

Her friend did a double take. "Uh, the *whole* night?"

She nodded.

"Like, sleeping until dawn, pass the milk, borrow your toothbrush—"

"Yeah, there was neither milk passing nor toothbrush borrowing, but it *was* dawn when he left."

Darla was silent a moment. "You sent him packing."

"Understatement." Her stomach rebelled at the memory of Beck's face after what she'd said. The lies she'd told to make him leave. Because what was the other option? Have him stay and do what? Eat pancakes? No. That wasn't her. Okay, she might have developed some murky feelings for the major, but they couldn't be more opposite. He was a relationship guy. She'd rather hear "Sweet Home Alabama" a fourth time. Sending Beck packing had done him a favor. Come Thursday morning, he could board the plane to Georgia with a clear conscience and some handy sexual experience. If she gave him any more encouragement, he might do something stupid. Like stay at Black Rock. For her. Which would make things much harder when he finally left. Because it would only be a matter of time.

No one stuck around forever.

"Can we drop it now?"

Darla lowered her glasses. "I haven't said anything in ten minutes."

"Huh." Kenna reached for her glass, but her hand froze in midair when Beck walked in. On cue, her thighs felt hot, her breasts heavy. The oxygen in her lungs seeped out like air from a tire. In faded jeans and a fitted navy blue T-shirt, he was the male equivalent of a triple fudge sundae with a cherry on top. Every man in the bar stood at least half a foot shorter, save the dark-haired man at his side who was also pretty tall, but still quite didn't reach Beck's height. *Shit*, she was staring at him like a certified goober. He hadn't seen her yet, thank Christ. She scooted into the shadows and ducked her head down. "He's here. He's here. Is there a back entrance?"

"Now there's a question a virgin would ask," Darla murmured. "He must have rubbed off on you."

"Save the comedy act. We're in full-on crisis mode."

Darla calmly sipped her drink. "Point him out to me before we steal into the night. I earned that by putting up with your twattage. I want to see the first man who managed to breach your apartment door."

Kenna dropped her head into her hands and groaned. "Blue T-shirt at the bar. You can't miss him, he's huge."

Her gaze scanned the crowd and stopped, mouth falling open. "How did *that* stay a virgin?"

"Long story involving a preacher's daughter and self-imposed abstinence." Jealousy over the two-timing Mary bubbled in the region of her midsection and she ground her teeth. "Can we go?"

"You're not going to introduce me?"

"Darla."

"Okay, fine." Darla scooted off the booth and stood. "You stay here lurking in the dark and I'll scout alternative exits."

She sent her friend a grateful look before hunkering down to wait.

* * *

The day was fast becoming the worst of Beck's life. And when you've lived through sandstorms and had tiny pieces of shrapnel removed in the field, that was definitely saying something. On the barstool next to him sat his best friend, Cullen Flanagan. They'd gone through boot camp together, side by side. Prior to shipping out, he'd asked Cullen to watch out for his sister, Huntley, while he was gone. Cullen had agreed without question. Beck's end of the bargain had been to look out for Xander Gibbons, one of Cullen's recruits and mentees. Beck had failed in that endeavor.

After Cullen had recruited Xander right out of Arizona State, the younger man had surprised no one when he'd followed in Cullen's impressive footsteps and chosen to specialize in EOD. Cullen had even submitted a request for Xander to train under him at Black Rock after he completed his basic training. The two really had been like brothers, hanging out after hours, too. Unfortunately, the fact that it had been Cullen to teach Xander how to properly disarm a bomb was the reason this conversation was so damn hard.

For six months Xander lived in Cullen's shadow, learning everything he could, but it hadn't been enough. As hard as this was on his friend, Beck knew it was only about to get harder.

"You've been back for two days?" Cullen tipped his bottle of Heineken back, his expression surly, which wasn't exactly breaking news. They didn't call him "Sullen Cullen" for nothing. Finishing his beer, he signaled for another. "You don't even stop by the warehouse to say hey? What have you been doing with yourself?"

Avoiding this painful conversation. Getting lost in a beautiful, fascinating girl who couldn't get enough or him one minute, and turned pricklier than a cactus the next.

Astute as usual, Cullen tilted his head and narrowed his eyes. "You meet someone, man?"

He started to say no, since he had no concrete answers when it came to Kenna, only shifting sand beneath his feet, but he couldn't deny his curiosity. Cullen would know of her, being that she was Sutton's daughter. Might be able to tell him something useful. Hell, maybe another part of him wanted to delay the world of hurt he was about to put Cullen in. "Yeah. I met someone." He shuffled the coaster between his hands on the bar. "Kenna Sutton."

Cullen choked on his beer. "Say again?"

"I'm guessing you know her," Beck said, trying to keep his voice even. Cullen was known for his reputation with women. If he'd spent time with Kenna, Beck didn't know how he'd react. Definitely not well. "If you've dated her, you best tell me now and get it out in the open, but I'm seeing her again, regardless, so watch what you say."

"Have I *dated* her?" Cullen laughed under his breath. "Are you serious?"

Beck's neck heated, right hand curling into a fist at what he deemed confirmation that Cullen and Kenna had been involved. *Breathe.* "Do I look serious?"

Cullen gave a rare smile. "Relax, man. They call her *No Men*-na Kenna. She's sealed up tighter than a nunnery at midnight." When Beck narrowed his gaze, Cullen signaled for shots. "Not that I've made any attempts to scale the nunnery walls. Tempting though she is."

Beck's body relaxed in degrees, temper cooling like he'd been doused in ice water. She'd lied to him? In an attempt to push him away, no doubt. Too bad it hadn't worked. Her past made no difference to him as long as he was in her present. Add to what he knew now—that Kenna's behavior toward him had been out of the ordinary—and his bone-deep feeling had been proven correct. This gravity he felt when they were together wasn't imaginary. She felt it too, dammit.

The wound in Beck's side demanded he shift positions. Cullen eyed him curiously as the shots were poured before them, but didn't comment. Beck left his shot untouched, but didn't object when Cullen motioned for anther round. This was it. A little fortification wouldn't hurt, and alcohol might help numb Cullen to the blow Beck was about to deliver.

No more putting it off. He'd had the trip home to digest how things went down over there, but it would be fresh for Cullen. As if Xander had just died.

"Beck!"

His sister's warm voice brought him up short. Until hearing her speak, he hadn't realized exactly how much he'd missed Huntley. He'd been away so long, concentrating on the job, staying alive…keeping others alive. After a while, missing his family had become an ache he'd learned to live with. An old injury. Having her familiar, smiling face so close made it new again. "Huntley." He stood and pulled her into a bear hug. "You look just the same."

"You look a touch meaner." She stepped back, wiping tears from her eyes. "When you helped get me this job here, I had this crazy idea you would be around. I'm so mad at you for being gone forever, I could smash something."

"Now that would be an interesting change," Cullen said behind him. "Your brother asked me to look out for you, but I can only check up on you at the library or coffeehouse so many times before I die of boredom."

She pursed her lips, but humor danced in her eyes. "Check out a book next time. You might learn something useful."

Cullen winked at her. "Curiosity killed the cat, sweetheart."

Beck wanted to stay quiet, observe this new dynamic between his best friend and once painfully shy sister. When she first arrived at Black Rock, Huntley hadn't been able to look at Cullen without turning red, but she'd apparently gotten over her shyness while Beck had been gone. If he could have sat there all night and left the news weighing down his shoulders for another time, he'd do it, no question, but the longer he waited, the harder it would be to get the words out.

"Huntley," Beck started, then immediately had to stop to clear his aching throat. "I didn't expect you tonight. There's something I need to speak with Cullen about. Let's meet tomorrow."

"You can't tell me whatever it is, too?" his sister asked, a flicker of hurt in her blue eyes. Rightly so, considering she was his twin and there had been a time they'd shared almost everything.

Cullen had gone still, except for his knuckles tapping

on the bar.

One of the drawbacks of going through basic training with someone meant there were no surprises. Beck's tone had been enough to warn the other man. "Had a feeling this wasn't just a friendly get-together."

Cullen inhaled and motioned for another round of shots. They were poured in swift order and he downed his glass in one motion. Beck didn't touch the one sitting in front of him, his gaze fastened to his friend. Cullen motioned at Beck's waiting glass. "You going to drink that?"

"I'm good, man," Beck replied, wincing when Cullen downed the hatch.

Huntley blinked at Cullen, disapproval beginning to color her expression. "I didn't realize we were getting drunk tonight."

"I didn't realize you needed to be consulted."

"Is that how you speak to my sister?" Taking a breath to allay his irritation, Beck shifted again to ease the pressure on his wound. "We'll have this discussion later."

Cullen continued to stare straight ahead, not a hint of emotion on his face. "It's about Xander, isn't it? You finally gonna tell me what happened over there?" A muscle ticked in his cheek. He gestured for another drink and watched impassively as it was poured. "When you called to tell us he wouldn't be coming home, I knew you were holding back. You're a shit liar, Beck. Out with it. How'd he die? What the hell happened over there?"

There would be no swaying his friend once stubbornness had set in, but dammit, he hadn't wanted an audience. Huntley and Cullen might be friends now, but Beck doubted he would want her to hear this. This was *Beck's* fault. He should have been more vigilant. If he'd fulfilled his promise to protect Xander, none of this would be happening. "If I could keep this from you forever, I would, because there's no sense in both of us feeling guilty, Cullen. But it's going to come out in the casualty report this week and I want it to come from me."

Both Huntley and Cullen remained very still.

Beck released a weary sigh. "We were extracting a group of POWs. They'd been there a week, but we couldn't get close enough or get an accurate count of the insurgents guarding them." He swallowed hard. "One of the POWs was a high-profile journalist and there was pressure to act faster than I felt comfortable with. We went in at night… and they'd moved locations through an underground tunnel. We missed them by mere minutes and when we entered the tunnel, there was an explosive device waiting for us." Cullen tensed beside him but maintained his hundred-yard stare. Beck closed his eyes, scenes from the tunnel bombarding him from all sides. "Xander was the most experienced specialist among us, but he—"

"Finish what you have to say," Cullen demanded, his voice quiet.

"He got it wrong." *Wood splintering, earth falling, shrapnel lodging in his side. Being unable to reach his friend.* "The explosive went off and half the tunnel caved in. Most of us were in an offshoot that remained standing." Huntley pressed her face to his shoulder and Beck wrapped an arm around her. "This isn't on you." *It's on me.* "No amount of training—"

Beck didn't even flinch when Cullen's fist shot out, sending the shot glasses crashing behind the bar because he'd known it was coming. Nor was he surprised when Cullen scraped back in his chair and took off toward the bar exit.

Beck started to go after Cullen, but Huntley, her eyes full of unshed tears, laid a hand on his arm. "I'll go." She rubbed her nose. "I'm a nurse. I work with grief-stricken soldiers every day. He thinks he's responsible, and that's worse than grief." She looked in the direction Cullen had gone, then back at Beck. "It's going to take him some time." Her blue eyes sharpened on him. Her hand reached out and touched his side through his shirt, as though assessing his injury. "I'm glad you're back and it's over, but you could have died over there, too, Beck. You're a part of me. I couldn't have handled that. Please don't keep anything like that from me again."

"I won't."

He only had a second to marvel over how strong his sister had become in his absence before she turned and went after Cullen. When the door of the bar slammed closed behind her, Beck felt it reverberate in his head, like a gunshot going off, telling him he shouldn't have come home. More than anything, he wished he'd made different judgment calls that would've resulted in having his friend home healthy. If such things were possible, he'd have switched places with Xander. *Too heavy.* The weight of that night, the things he'd heard and seen, was a two-hundred-pound anvil tied to his neck.

Without having made a conscious decision, Beck pushed back from the bar, his destination already a foregone conclusion in his mind. Kenna. Her name was synonymous with comfort, with losing himself, being taken to a place where he didn't have to think or hurt. He tossed a handful of bills onto the bar and started to leave, but a prickle at the back of his neck gave him pause. Were his eyes playing tricks on him? No. There she stood, about halfway down the bar. Another girl tugged on her arm, urging her in the opposite direction, but Kenna wasn't budging. She watched him, an odd expression on her face.

Beck didn't second-guess himself. He went for her.

# CHAPTER EIGHT

*Oh mama.* Kenna had two hundred and fifty pounds of muscle heading her way and it was attached to intensity so thick it surrounded her legs so they couldn't move. Why hadn't she followed Darla out the back exit? She'd *started* to, but the misery radiating from Beck had reached her from the bar. At once, his cryptic explanation from their first afternoon together had replayed, as if she was hearing them for the first time. *What I came back with, what I failed to do…it'll be a burden on everyone soon enough.*

Burdened. That's exactly what he'd looked like as first his friend, and then the woman so obviously related to him had bailed, leaving him there. She didn't know what bomb he'd dropped, but knew one thing with total certainty. Beck wasn't a man who caused others pain if he could damn well help it. She couldn't be the third person to walk away from him that night. It didn't seem fair. Fair. *Right.* That was the only reason she was standing there, no doubt resembling a wigged-out forest creature who had heard a twig snap.

When Beck had almost reached her, she managed a paltry step backward, but it was too late. He stooped down to wrap a brawny arm behind her hips, lifting her against his hard body with so little effort, a whimper snuck out. His friend sending shot glasses flying across the bar had garnered zero attention, but Lieutenant General Sutton's daughter being manhandled in public grinded the entire operation to a halt. The band forgotten, everyone shuffled around to face them. Thankfully, the music was still loud enough that only Kenna—and Darla, who stood openmouthed beside her—could make out Beck's words.

"I *need* you," he growled against her parted mouth.

Was she nodding? Yes. Yes, she was. *Stop.* "N-need me?"

"Yeah." He straightened to his full height and her feet left the floor, leaving her tummy somewhere in the vicinity of his boots. "I was mad this morning. Too mad to say my peace. I'm going to say it now. You listening?"

She swung her feet where they dangled in the air. "Uh-huh."

"Good." He laid a hard kiss on her lips. A series of gasps and laughter erupted around them. Beck, although seemingly oblivious to the scene they were creating, pressed his mouth to her ear and dropped his voice. "You might have been my first, Kenna, but I'm a grown man with a brain and a heart. And I know it isn't going to feel like that with just anyone. I *know.*" His arm tightened around her, crushing her even harder against his body. "Now, you're going to walk out of here holding my hand."

"I don't hold hands," she breathed, staunchly ignoring the flip-flop in her chest cavity.

"You hold *my* hand." In direct contradiction of his

harshly delivered command, he kissed her temple with devastating gentleness. "You hold *my* hand, darlin'."

Oh mama, indeed. The way he was making her feel—like she'd fallen into a warm, racing current of water—was very bad.

"Well." Kenna heard the jingle of Darla's keys to her left. "Excuse me while I go home and weep into a pint of Chunky Monkey while lamenting my lack of strapping young suitors."

Kenna's mouth fell open as her friend deserted her, but Beck recaptured her attention. "So I walk out of here holding your hand. And…and then what?"

Beck settled her on her feet and took her hand. "We go somewhere and talk."

"Talk," she said dazedly, already craving the feel of his spectacular body again. "Right."

Customers parted as Beck led her out of the bar. And damn if his lack of interest in the gaping crowd didn't attract her even more. As far back as her earliest memory, she'd been a fixture on base and no one had ever deemed her worth the trouble of pissing off her father. Or dealing with the antics of her teenage years, for which she'd become notorious. It alarmed her that she still didn't have this man pegged. Shouldn't a well-mannered, aspiring peach farmer from Georgia care about incurring her father's wrath?

The cool night air felt like perfection against her flushed skin as they entered the dark parking lot, but her relief was short-lived. Beck strode toward her car and since he had a bear grip on her hand, she had no choice but to stumble after him. "I tasted bourbon when I kissed you. Were you planning on drinking and driving?"

"No," she drew out. "Darla was my ride and she doesn't drink."

"Tonight, neither did I. Cough up your keys."

She ground to a halt. "No one drives that car but me."

Beck spun her around, wedging her backside against the driver's side door. The second his body touched hers, she went totally pliant, the air whooshing from her lungs. *Grab me, touch me, take me.* Instead of doing any of those things, Beck tilted his head as if perplexed by Kenna's reaction. "You're either spitting fire or turning sweet on me." She felt his half smile down to her toes. "I'm starting to think you're fighting the same battle I am."

Aw, hell. That definitely wasn't his belt buckle pressing against her stomach. *No sudden movements.* "What battle would that be?"

He braced his hands on the car's roof, stretching the T-shirt across his mountain range of muscle. When her diminished willpower gave her no choice but to memorize the sight, he made a sound like, *huh.* Perfect. The ex-virgin had become self-aware. "The battle not to pick you up and drop you down on my hard-on. *That* battle."

Heavy heat spread between her legs, assaulting her senses. "Oh, that one," she whispered.

He dragged his body against her, side to side. "Yeah."

"I, um…" Her neck lost power, sending her head falling back. "I thought you wanted to talk."

"Oh, we're getting there." Beck trailed his open mouth over her ear, breathing into her hair. "Today hasn't been my best, Kenna. Put your hands on me and make me forget."

His husky plea plucked a string inside of her and it went against her nature to deny him comfort. She couldn't withstand the draw. Not after the expression of defeat she'd seen on his face inside the bar. Her fingers moved on their own, tracing the waistband of his jeans, across the tight planes of his stomach that hollowed beneath her touch. Hungry with the need to please him, she smoothed her palms up his ridged torso, dragging her nails down over his nipples once she reached the top.

"*God*," he groaned, his callused hands fisting in the hem of her skirt. "I know how to make you come now. Know you like it rough. Just *let* me." He wedged his thigh between her legs. Using the hem of her skirt for leverage, Beck rocked her forward, making her moan. "This is what I see now when you walk around in these short pieces of nothing that hug your ass. I see something I can twist my hands in. Something I can lift just an inch or two and see the too-tight pussy I'm already an addict for. You've done this to me in *two days*, and I can't go back to seeing this as just a skirt. Or think of you as a one-night stand. I can't go back to *not* fucking you."

"Yes. Okay. *Yes*." She clutched his broad shoulders and bucked her hips, riding the hard length of his thigh. Her inhibitions and any semblance of rational thought pulled a Houdini, and she couldn't care less as long as he kept touching her. Kept talking. Warning bells were pealing somewhere in the distance telling her this was the point of no return, but she didn't heed them. Couldn't. "Please, Beck. Let's go somewhere."

"Thank Christ." He dropped his forehead onto her shoulder. "I thought you were done with me."

Kenna's equilibrium pitched. *Apparently not done yet.* Apprehension twined with the desire that still ran rampant.

This undeniable need was new and terrifying, but she didn't have the ability to deny him. He made her feel too…right. Like she was supposed to be here all along and hadn't known.

"Keys," he prompted, brushing the hair away from her face. "I'm driving."

"Just this once," she said, wondering if her words had a double meaning. Could she open herself up, just this once? He was leaving in a matter of days. Maybe that was her excuse to abandon caution. No matter what happened tonight, the inevitable would happen and he'd go away. Jesus, if he left tonight, she didn't think getting over their time together would be so simple. Why not add one more memory before she was forced to recover?

* * *

Beck felt Kenna's smirk as he crouched down to fit inside the car, the steering wheel digging into his chest until he moved the seat back to its farthest setting. Trying not to be obvious, he released a pent-up breath, nice and slow. He'd taken a gamble bossing her around. Truth be told, he'd half expected her to slap him across the face. Everything he'd said had been true, however. Starting with the fact that he *needed* her. Tonight. And *after* tonight.

He felt raw and ripped open after hurting Cullen, knowing it would be a long time coming before he could move forward. If words existed that would ease what Cullen was feeling, he'd go after him. But he knew from experience, Cullen had already shut the world—including him—out. Huntley would shift the focus. Tomorrow, once they'd gotten their heads together, he'd find a way to set healing in motion for Cullen.

Right now, though? Right now, he needed Kenna to suture his wounds. Seeing her in the dim, dusty bar had been enough to put him back on solid ground, but more was needed. All of her. Accomplishing that required him to play the long game, which meant making this impromptu date last longer than it would take them to have sex. Long enough to talk. Ah, Christ. If he wanted to do this right, he couldn't even think the word *sex* with her in the vicinity.

Starting now.

Beside him, she crossed her legs, treating Beck to a glimpse of her smooth, inner thigh.

Okay…starting now.

Kenna arched her back on the seat, sighing as he started the car. His dick felt strangled inside his pants. If he asked, would she stroke it while he drove?

*Dammit.* Starting now? Right.

"Where are you going to take me?"

The way she purred the double-meaning question meant she knew all about his agony—and enjoyed it. "Somewhere public where you can't tempt me."

"Aw, that's no fun."

He threw his arm over the passenger seat, backing her car out of its spot. "We're having a conversation, Kenna."

"Yes, I got that." She rubbed her cheek against his bicep. "How about this? I'll take you somewhere private—" Her hand came up when he attempted to interrupt. "Now hear me out. I promise not to touch you until the conversation portion of the evening has been completed to your satisfaction."

"I know when I'm being patronized." She grinned

and the distraction almost made Beck hit a parked car, but he slammed on the brakes at the last second. "How am I supposed to tell you no with a smile like that aimed at me?"

Ironically, his words made her smile waver. "Take a right turn out of the parking lot."

Beck ignored the pang in his middle and followed her directions. If he let her reticence bother him, they'd have another scene like that morning, which would only damage his cause. Fortunately, when they reached the checkpoint leading onto base and the soldiers on patrol reacted with shock to see Kenna with him, his irritation vanished. According to Cullen, she didn't date on base, yet here they were. *One victory at a time.*

They'd only been on base two minutes when she pointed through the windshield. "See the brick building up ahead? Turn in there."

"The physical therapy center?" He slowed the car down. "It's not open at night."

"I know." She sent him a sly look. "I have keys."

Of course she did. "How's that?"

Her voice turned solemn. "After my father's heart attack, I brought him here for therapy sessions. He thought it made him look weak, so I brought him during off hours. Sometimes he'd just swim, which didn't require the doctor." She shrugged. "They forgot to take the keys back."

Beck's mind was busy cataloguing what she'd revealed, not just about her relationship with the lieutenant general, but simply by the sad way she spoke about him. So busy, a slightly more pressing detail occurred to him only after they'd parked the car in the deserted lot. "And what are *we* doing here?"

Kenna pushed open the passenger side door. "Don't be a surprise ruiner, Major."

With a fortifying breath for what he was about to face, Beck climbed out. "I hate surprises."

She stopped short at the bumper. "Me too. Maybe we have something in common after all." Before he could address her implication that they only had one thing in common, she sailed toward the building. "Anyway, turnabout is fair play, since you surprised me the day we met." With a jingle of her keys, the center's door swung open. "I'm merely returning the favor."

"*You* were surprised?" Beck asked, following her into the darkened lobby. "I expected a wet-behind-the-ears new recruit to pick me up. Instead, I get you." He couldn't resist skimming her body with a heated look, noticing the way her nipples beaded under his regard. *Stop staring or you'll fail.* "In terms of surprises, I won the day."

"You might have me there." She gazed up at him from beneath her eyelashes. "Considering the way it ended and all."

The memory of Kenna on her knees, taking his cock to the back of her throat, burned him from the inside. He tightened his fists in order to avoid grabbing her. God, she *knew* he was struggling. Her confident stride moved her ass in a way that dried his mouth. Left to right, over and back, beneath that utterly liftable skirt. *Sweet hell.* He'd set himself up for disaster, hadn't he? Their footsteps echoed on the linoleum floor of the hallway, breaking off when she paused in front of a fogged glass door. Beck didn't allow their bodies to touch, but couldn't resist bracing his hands on the doorframe as she worked the lock, leaning down to smell her hair.

He smiled when she nearly dropped the keys. "You got a thing for my shampoo, True Blue?"

"I've got a thing for just about every part of you."

"Well, then." She nudged open the door and flipped on the overhead light. "That bodes well for tonight's plan."

Beck's gaze scanned the massive room, narrowing on the in-ground hot tub Kenna was heading toward in the corner. With a sense of impending doom, Beck kicked the door shut, flipped the lock and followed, noting the lap pool to the left, adjacent to the hot tub. Off to the right was a tiled area where doctors performed therapy sessions. Oversized leather tables where he himself had been stretched after a hamstring injury during basic training, sat in a neat row, although the facility had certainly been upgraded since he'd been there.

*Nice try, thinking about the new showers and sturdier tables.* Anything to distract him from Kenna toeing off her boots by the edge of the water. Or the look she was sending him over her shoulder that said *help me get these pesky clothes off, big guy.*

"I reckon you think this is funny," he said, voice gone gruff. There was no choice but to close the short distance between them, his body magnetized by hers. Kenna stripped her shirt off in response, but didn't turn, so all he could see was her bare back. Although, he would go to the grave swearing a sexier back had never existed. Not on this earth. "You enjoy testing me, is that it?"

"Yes." She hooked her fingers in the sides of her skirt and turned, giving him a mind-blowing view of her partially naked body. "I love testing you. I love it even more when you give in."

The skirt hit the floor and Beck heaved a breath, reeling at the speed of which his body reacted. He'd seen her without clothes, but she'd been up close. From a distance, he could take her all in at once. Words hadn't been invented yet to describe her curves, the angles of her hips and tits. In a word, she was devastation. And she'd just declared war.

"Get in," he croaked, crossing to the control panel on the wall.

Watching him curiously, she stepped into the warm tub and sank beneath the surface. When Beck turned on the bubbles a second later, obscuring her luscious body from his view, she nodded. "Well played."

*Darlin', you haven't seen anything yet.* Back in the bar parking lot, she'd tipped her hand and now he knew the rampant attraction wasn't one-sided. The girl had dropped her guard and given him a weapon. He might have been shocked to realize that weapon was him, but he wouldn't hesitate to use it. Hyperaware of her lingering attention, Beck took hold of his T-shirt and whipped it over his head, tossing it toward her pile of clothes where they lay in a heap on the tile. He unbuckled his belt, sliding it through the loops, before going to work on his zipper. Their eyes locked, and he noted hers had turned a darker shade of green, a perfect complement to the pink traveling over her cheeks.

The hot tub's hum failed to mask her sharp intake of breath when Beck's jeans landed at his feet, allowing his dick to bob against his stomach.

"Okay." Kenna fell back against the submerged wall. "Not so funny now."

# CHAPTER NINE

Kenna whispered a heartfelt goodbye as Beck's impressive erection disappeared beneath the water's surface. Even though Beck had made it clear he wanted them to talk, she still couldn't believe it when he sat on the underwater bench, which happened to be a good five feet away. She was frustrated, yes. There was no denying her libido had blasted off like the space shuttle when his pants came off, but damn was she turned on by more than his physique. A man who knew how to use the head downstairs while still thinking with the one on his shoulders? Yeah. Those were limited edition. Throw in the way he looked at her, like he couldn't wait to see what she said next? Hey. He'd sunk Kenna's battleship.

She'd known he was capable of it, so why had she brought him here? Agreed to spend time with him? Because he'd looked so lost at Bombs Away. As if the world had shaken under his feet and he couldn't find balance. Remembering the expression that had rooted her in place when she should have been running for the back exit, Kenna felt selfish for attempting to seduce him. Obviously he needed someone to talk to, and she couldn't see past her own insecurities. *You suck.*

"What happened back at Bombs Away?" His head came up, but he stayed silent. Kenna hugged her elbows, completely out of her comfort zone in this hot tub heart-to-heart. "Something to do with that man and your sister, maybe? You looked unhappy."

"How did you know she was my sister?"

Kenna decided not to impart the sharp sting of jealousy she'd experienced before noticing the resemblance. "You said she worked on base, she has the same shade of dirty blond hair…and you both dip your chin when someone else is talking."

When she demonstrated the move, his lips twitched. "You've been watching me almost as closely as I've been watching you, Kenna." His eyebrows drew together. "The three of us came to Black Rock at the same time, but there was a fourth until two months ago. Xander Gibbons. He didn't make it home." He stared down into the fizzing water. "They tell me there's nothing I could have done, but I *know*. I could have saved a good man. Besides Huntley, he was the best of us."

"I'm sorry." The steam rose around them, partially obscuring him from sight. "I won't try and convince you it wasn't your fault, even though it wasn't. You're the type to shoulder the world, no matter the cause, but I'm so sorry you lost your friend."

She could see he wanted to believe her—wanted to let her absolve him—but wasn't quite ready. "Is this why you left with me tonight? Were you feeling bad for me?"

Why would that upset him? "That was part of it."

Beck looked away. "The first time you came to me, you felt bad because I had no one to welcome me home. After dinner at your father's…" His laughter was strained. "I was ready to beg for you that night, Kenna. We both knew how much pain I was in to be inside your body."

"I don't understand where this is going."

He moved. Before she could blink, Beck was right in front of her, water lapping against his shoulders. Kenna's pulse skittered in her veins as heat exploded between them. "Are you here with me because you want to nurture me? Or because you feel better when I'm close?" He dipped his head, granting her mouth the barest of contact. "And because you want this dick."

Kenna bit back a whimper. "I'm not a nurturer. You have the wrong girl if you think that."

He shook his head, dragging his lips across hers. "I call it like I see it. You might have done a damn fine job hiding it, but I see right through you."

"I'm here because I feel better when you're close," she blurted in a furious whisper, scared that if he continued his thought, she'd have to acknowledge the truth behind his words.

Her rushed admission drew different reactions from each of them. Beck looked relieved while Kenna knew shock coated her expression. Had she actually admitted that out loud?

"Let's hear the rest, Kenna."

Mist from the hot water bathed her lips and she licked it off, giving herself time to calm her out-of-control heartbeat. It didn't work. She pressed her forehead to his shoulder.

"I'm here because I want your dick."

Beck growled, his tongue traced a path over her ear. "You're going to get it soon enough."

She had no time to brace herself before he sank back into the water, putting space between them once again. "You've got to be kidding me."

The obvious misery on Beck's face made her feel only marginally better. "Why did I get the feeling you weren't welcome in your father's house?" A muscle in his cheek ticked. "I didn't like it."

The change of topic had her head spinning. "Wait. What?" Hadn't they been talking about his dick seconds ago? "*This* is what you wanted to talk about?"

He nodded once. "Among other things."

She wanted to blow off the line of questioning, but a glance toward the pool had her remembering all the times she'd woken up at the crack of dawn to drive her father to physical therapy. Half the time, she'd passed out on one of the leather benches until he'd finished swimming and wanted to leave, but it had made her feel useful. Like she'd made a difference in his recovery. "I'm welcome there. I just…" *I've served my purpose.* "You don't know what I was like before. It's a wonder they'll bring me around polite company at all." When Beck only watched her with quiet patience, she sliced a hand through the water. "Aren't you going to ask me what I was like before?"

"I don't care about before. I care about now."

Kenna stared. "Why do you care at all, Beck? Shouldn't it tell you something that my own parents have moved on and done their best to forget the portion of their life that includes me? They would erase me if they could. I'm a necessary evil to them."

"No." His harsh tone brought to mind the metal she worked with. "I don't believe that."

"You probably believe there's good in everyone," she continued as if he hadn't spoken. "That's you. Discarding people is a foreign idea when you're a big, fat war hero."

"I'm no hero, Kenna."

She scoffed. "I've been here a long time. I can separate out the good men, and you're one of them. It's why you can't just let me go."

He didn't look happy. At all. "Explain that statement."

Fear dripped slowly into her chest. Fear that once she outlined the reality for him, he'd see the truth in her explanation and bail. "My mother trapped my father into marriage by getting pregnant. She worked herself to the bone trying to earn his love and it never happened. Never. He doesn't have it in him to love someone. His relationship with Tina is all about convenience." She sucked in a breath. "I represent failure to both of them. My mom thought I could fix what was broken in my father, and I couldn't. My father sees me as a product of his one and only fuck-up. Now he only makes room for me in his life when it's convenient." Her laughter held no trace of humor. "And yet, here I am. Living within walking distance of them both, wondering when I'll see them next, like some masochist. The truth is, they found something better."

"You're not a masochist. You want them to love you the same way you love them." Kenna didn't realize he'd come closer until he cupped the side of her face. "You still haven't explained why I can't let you go."

Common sense commanded she push him away.

This closeness was too personal and he saw too much, but she couldn't move under the intensity of his focus on her. It surrounded her like a hot whirlpool. "There are a few reasons."

He caressed her bottom lip with his thumb, appearing fascinated by the curved feature. "Let's hear them, so I can shoot them down one by one."

"You've gotten a lot more confident since we first met."

Beneath the water, their bodies brushed. "I managed to get the beautiful girl to come back for more. That does something to a man."

*Holy shit*, she was turning into a straight-up junkie for his touch. The flesh at the juncture of her thighs contracted, seeking fulfillment. From him. Only him. Still… "We're two different types of people, Beck. You ring the doorbell to meet your date's father. I climb out my window and hitchhike to Florida while everyone's sleeping."

His sculpted lips lifted at one end. "You're worth shaking hands over. Worth the time it takes to be read the riot act, Kenna. I'll always be the guy who wants to show you that." He dropped a hand beneath the bubbling water and stroked her belly with his knuckles. "That doesn't mean I won't choose to show you a different way once we're alone. And darlin', I wouldn't make it to Florida before that happened. Not even half a mile."

An image of her straddling Beck in the backseat of a car made her short of breath. "Not everyone needs a hero, Beck. Not everyone wants to be repaired."

"Good. Because you're not broken." He gave her a hard look. "I'm sorry the people who love you made you feel that way. They're the ones who need fixing."

The precipice beneath her feet had nearly corroded, so she played her trump card. "You're leaving. Going back to Georgia."

"You let me worry about that right now." His stare didn't waver. "Don't think about it tonight."

Not so impossible when he appeared intent on consuming her thoughts. "What do you want me to think about instead?"

Beck slid his knuckles down her belly, over her mound to rub them between her legs. "I can tell you what I'm thinking about." His breath bathed her damp forehead. "You told me nothing we do is wrong. Does that extend to my mouth, darlin'?"

"Yes," she breathed.

"Thank God." He ground his closed fist against her core and she gasped. "Kenna…I'm thinking I fucked this and now its mine." She swayed forward and landed against his wet chest. "Before I met you, saying those words would have horrified me," he grated at her ear. "But when my dick gets hard to be inside your body, I don't second-guess anything. When we're not fucking, I will treat you like gold. But right now, all I can think about is wearing out my little bad girl. I want to carry your limp body out of here in my goddamn arms. Do you understand me?"

He pushed two fingers into her pulsing heat, ripping a gasp from her lips. It felt so unbelievably *good.* "I-I guess that means we're done talking."

* * *

*My girl. Mine.*

A category five hurricane tore through Beck and he didn't bother trying to weather it or minimize the damage. He'd considered himself a reasonable, generous man. A man who saw everything from an objective standpoint. Yet there was no objectivity when it came to Kenna. He wanted to give and take so many things from her, all at once. Wanted to give pleasure, security, reassurance. And he wasn't too proud a man to admit he wanted those things from her in return.

He looked down into her upturned face and saw the final brick in her wall tumble to the ground, leaving nothing more between them. Good Lord. She had no idea that her guard falling had sealed her fate, did she? Before she'd confided all her secrets, he'd already fallen for her, but the vulnerable girl she'd revealed called to the protector in him. His muscles ached with the need to go to battle for her. Protect her. Make her feel worthy, the way she'd done for him. And *God*, he was possessive. If she only knew how badly he wanted to beat his chest right now at having won her trust, would it scare her? No. No, she'd tell him nothing he felt pressed to do was wrong. Another reason he wouldn't be letting her go. She accepted every damn thing about him.

Emotion built in his throat until he had no choice but to stop staring at her gorgeous face and kiss her. Her pussy tightened around his fingers when their tongues licked together. *Christ*. The knowledge his mouth on hers could affect her between the legs rocked him, encouraged him to deepen the kiss. She undulated her hips, riding his fingers as he drew them in and out. So warm and wet. Someday soon he would make her come into his palm, but not now. The driving need to be inside her, have her body wrapped around him, demanded satisfaction. His hoarse groan must have betrayed his thoughts because Kenna's hand found his cock, stroking it beneath the water.

"Harder," he ground out. "Rough and fast. The way I'm going to take you."

"*Yes*," she moaned. "That's what I need."

Beck rose from the water and savored the sight of her beneath him on the seat, her hand eagerly working his cock. Redness suffused her cheeks, mouth falling open as she perused him, head to toe. As he reached for his pants on the tile behind her to retrieve a newly purchased condom, her green eyes roamed over his pectorals and stomach before landing where he wanted them, on his heavy erection. It swelled larger under her regard while he applied the latex.

She moistened her lips. "You're sexy as hell, Beck. You know that?"

Surprise laced through the lust. He'd known she was attracted to him, but to hear it straight from her mouth made him confident and desperate at the same time. Unable to battle his baser urges any longer, he banged his fist against his chest. "Stand up and climb on then."

Water traveled down her body in streams as she stood on the seat, passing over her pointed nipples, her flat stomach...*fuck*, her bare pussy. Beck found himself jealous of the water itself. Nothing should touch her but him. She dug her fingers into his shoulders and slid up his body, legs wrapping around his waist like a vise. Beck's head fell back on a moan when she reached behind her and led his cock to her slippery entrance. "I'm going to ride you so hard." She licked up his neck, sending a wave of heat straight to his groin. "All you have to do is watch."

When she eased down on his length, Beck moaned long and loud. Couldn't help it. The perfect tightness of her combined with her open-mouthed expression of pleasure blew any other experience in his life right out of the water.

"You know what's so hot," she whispered, giving a slow buck of her hips and releasing a shaky breath. "You could walk around with me like this all day without breaking a sweat."

"Damn right." A shudder passed through him. "Part of me would love it, too. Letting you milk me everywhere I go."

She lifted and swiveled her body on the way back down. "What about the other part of you?"

Beck was fast losing focus on anything but the spot their bodies connected, but he pressed their foreheads together, making sure she was looking him in the eye. "The other part of me already wants to kill anyone who will covet what's mine."

Her breathing grew choppy. "You fucked this, now it's yours?"

"That's right," he growled, his hands lifting to grip her flexing thighs, barely restraining himself from throwing her down and thrusting until she screamed. "I'm giving you one minute to play, Kenna, then it's time to start wearing you out. I'll be making up for lost time with that sinner's body."

"Yes, Beck." Holding on to his shoulders, she leaned back and gave him an earth-shaking view of her writhing body, the spot where his cock appeared and disappeared into her smooth pussy. Around him, her legs increased their hold as she began sliding up and down his length. Her addicting whimpers were almost carried away by the frothing water, but he grabbed and savored them. The faster she moved, the more his sanity threatened to desert him. Needing her close, he crushed her against his chest, taking her mouth in a punishing kiss even as she continued riding his sensitive dick. *Can't hold off any longer.* He needed to pin her, gain leverage. Thrust as hard as possible.

Without knowing if her minute had expired—and no longer giving a damn—Beck waded toward the hot tub steps, climbing out of the water while Kenna continued to buck and moan, nails digging into his shoulders. Jesus, he loved the pain. It proved she was real and not a trick of his imagination.

His attention snagged on a mirrored wall, stretching along one end of the physical therapy area. The sight of Kenna clinging to him, her back and ass rolling sensually, nearly brought him to his knees. *Closer.* He had to get closer. See the perfection of her up close while experiencing the heaven of her wet heat taking him shallow and deep. Shallow and deep. Teeth gritted, Beck crossed the room at a brisk stride, stopping in front of the mirror. "Damn. *Damn*, Kenna. Look at you." He gripped her right ass cheek—watched the reflection of his hand squeezing the flesh below her sexy barbed wire tattoo—until she cried out. "If I'd known you existed, coming in my own hand would have been fucking impossible. All those years..." He threw his head back on a groan. "Nothing would have compared. I would have been miserable without your pussy."

She started to put on a show then. Watching his face as she treated him to a hot bump and grind, her body glistening in the muted light. "The way you squeeze my ass. It's like you're trying to prevent yourself from doing more with that hand."

There was a heady truth behind her words. A desire he struggled to acknowledge because he'd pushed it so deep, ignored it for so long. He took her mouth in a furious kiss, pulling away only when air was required. But even that delicious distraction couldn't tear his mind away from the invitation in her voice. "What do you mean by something more?"

Her eyes were bright, her voice seductive. "You want to spank me, Beck?"

# CHAPTER TEN

The breath fled Kenna's lungs as Beck lifted her off his stiff arousal and whirled her around. He hadn't responded to her question, but his expression had been answer enough. Just when she thought all of Beck's layers had been peeled back, another was revealed and she loved it. Loved being the one to liberate his repressed sexual nature. A nature that was turning out to be insatiable and filthy. To her, sex had always been enjoyable, but tended to feel choreographed. Nothing about sex with Beck felt planned—it was down and dirty, honest-to-God slaking of lust. Nothing felt off limits. And for someone like Kenna, who didn't open up easily, it was *freeing*. Like she'd taken flight for the first time.

She faced away from Beck now, her stomach pressed against the edge of a leather therapy table, made slippery from her dripping body. His restraint was obvious as he breathed heavily into her hair, hands flexing at her hips. "I don't lay hands on women," he said, voice like gravel.

Exulting in the privilege of being the one to correct his

misconception, give him the extra push, Kenna flattened her palms on the table, bent forward and tilted her hips. As if he had no control over his actions, Beck dragged his hard cock up and down the valley of her bottom, making her moan. "This is for my pleasure, Beck." She tossed her hair, meeting his tortured gaze over her shoulder. "Don't you want to give me pleasure?"

"Yes. *Constantly*."

"Then take yours and watch me find mine, too."

She leaned down and pressed her cheek to the cool leather, her face turned so she could watch him in the mirror. His barrel chest shuddered once, twice, his right hand lifting and flexing in the air. Finally, as if the final barrier had crumbled, his huge hand landed on her backside with a satisfying *slap*. "Oh, God," she breathed, the flesh between her legs tightening like a fist. Beck's erection bulged against her backside, telling her without words how affected he'd been. Her vision cleared and she saw him in the mirror, watching her with a mixture of concern and arousal. Sweat had broken out on his forehead, the muscles in his arms straining beneath his skin. *Fuck hot*. "That made me feel so good, Beck." She licked the saltiness from her lips. "Did you like it?"

"Too much." His voice had dropped to such a deep pitch, it set off a dark, dangerous throb beneath her belly button. "I'm not sure about the things it made me feel…the things I want to do."

Kenna started to remind him nothing they did was wrong, but his hand colliding with her still-damp backside had her gasping instead.

"I know what you're going to say. That nothing

between us is wrong," he grated, smacking her buttocks with increased force. "What if I *want* it to feel a little wrong, darlin'. What then?"

Turned on to a level she'd never encountered, it became difficult to get air into her lungs. Was that *her* making the table shake? "It'll only be wrong if you stop."

In the space of two seconds, he'd fisted his erection, guided the thick head to her entrance and plunged every merciless inch inside her, roaring as he went. Kenna screamed into the table's leather surface but was cut off when he started to drive himself home, again and again. The buildup had been so great, the anticipation so intense, an orgasm stripped her from the inside out. It seemed never ending, bolstered by Beck filling her to capacity with each thrust. The table rocked beneath her, its wooden legs scraping on the ground, but Beck grabbed it by the sides and held it still, kept it from moving forward. Pinned. She was pinned at the hips by his swollen arousal and the knowledge was indescribable.

Kenna thought the force of Beck entering her couldn't get any greater, but she was wrong. He used his white-knuckled grip on the table to jerk her—*and the table*—back, to meet his drives. *Scrape, scrape, scrape.* She became part of the heavy piece of furniture, bent over its edge, existing to service him. Behind her, Beck growled, the sound mingling with the scrape of wood on tile. "You need this, don't you, Kenna? Need my cock to be the only one that gets you from now on?" He moved faster. *Faster.* "That's what *I* need."

Her muffled reply got lost in the sound of wet flesh connecting. She had no idea what her response had been, anyway. Didn't care. Could only concentrate on the pleasure teasing her loins, getting ready to go off like a camera flash. Almost there. *Almost there.*

Abruptly, Beck ceased his tireless drives, removing one hand from the table to reach between her legs. "You need me to touch you here, don't you? I'm a fast learner, Kenna." The callused pads of his fingers dragged over her clit, then circled, his hips delivering deliberate, slow thrusts. "I watched every move you made our first night. I know you like when I use my size against you. When I bounce you up and down like a little doll." His fingers moved faster, rougher. "And now I know a good slap on your perked-up ass gets you the wettest of all, don't I?"

To emphasize his point, he pulled out until only the tip of his arousal remained inside her, then slammed back inside, demanding an answer. "*Yes!*"

"I know *everything* you need. *Everything.*" His chest aligned with her back, pressing her down into the leather table, his stubble rasping over her ear. "*I'm* your daddy now, Kenna."

The force of her climax ripped a scream from her lips, the sound bouncing off the tile floor and echoing throughout the room. Her fingernails clawed at the leather, struggling to gain purchase, even though she never would again. She was given no time to process Beck's words or their impact on her before he gripped the table's sides once more and heaved her backward onto his waiting erection. Once, twice, three times, before shoving to the deepest recesses of her womanhood and loosing a primitive shout. One that made her feel claimed—owned—as he came. Beck's body was wracked with tremors that vibrated through her when his huge frame collapsed onto her back.

She listened to the sound of their labored breaths with

exhausted fascination. Had she known the moment she saw Beck that he would be important to her? If she thought back, it seemed undeniable and he'd just proven it. Thoroughly. What would compare to this? This feeling of depleted exultancy? Nothing. He'd asked her not to worry about his leaving tonight and in her current state, she had no choice. She wanted to forget about it for the night, leave it in his hands. *I know everything you need. Everything.* The independent woman at her core loathed that sentiment, until it had been spoken by Beck. Now she loved it, because it went both ways. Hadn't he said he needed *her* back in the bar?

"Take me home," she whispered, sighing when he kissed her damp neck.

"I'll always take you home," he said. "But this time, you stay in bed with me until we're both ready to get up. I don't wake up alone this time."

It was an actual effort to nod. "Okay."

He lifted her onto the leather table where she curled up on her side as Beck went to retrieve their clothes. After treating her to the sight of him dressing, Beck replaced her panties, slipping her skirt back up her legs with a gentleness that made her chuckle after the way he'd just taken her. He watched her closely as she pulled on her tank top. As soon as she was dressed, Beck lifted her into his arms and carried her pliant body from the building.

• • •

Beck glanced back at Kenna where she slept, her hair a dark, tangled mess on the pillow. The skirt and tank top she'd worn home last night were somewhere back in the living room, he reckoned, leaving her sweet body exposed on top of the twisted sheets. God, she was so damn pretty. If he didn't think it would creep her out, he could watch her sleep for hours.

How many times last night had he loved her? So many times it felt like a disjointed dream. Hands, mouths, Kenna's screams, his answering shouts, the bed creaking. Those legs of hers. They'd been shoved open, wrapped around him, pushed up near her ears, bruised by the force of his grip. In the sunlight, those light discolorations made a hard lump form in his throat, but it eased upon remembering her encouragement. The way she'd begged for him to go harder. *Harder.*

With considerable effort, Beck turned back around, hands clasped between his knees where he sat on the edge of the bed.

Yeah. Saying the two of them had good chemistry was a woeful understatement. She was necessity now. His safe place, the keeper of his desire. And now that she'd let her guard down, he could barely keep up with the things she made him feel. Protectiveness, awe…happiness. At some point last night, when they'd been catching their breath, her soft voice had reached him across the pillow. *Tell me about your peach farm.*

From that point on, they'd talked for hours about his time overseas, her love of welding, only stopping when his cock started to feel heavy, a condition she'd been all too eager to relieve. Just remembering her mouth skating down his torso was questioning his decision not to take her again this morning. Rolling her body over so he could get at that tight pussy.

*Damn.*

But no, he wouldn't. Decisions needed to be made, and they didn't have time to pretend his plane to Georgia wasn't leaving bright and early tomorrow morning. He had loose ends to tie up before the ceremony tonight, Cullen and his sister to face. Confronting any of it would be impossible without the assurance that he'd have Kenna on the other side. His hands shook at the very possibility that he might not. That she'd wake up and throw her barriers back up, blocking him out.

Beck heard Kenna shift behind him and turned. Ah, Jesus. He hadn't been prepared for the sight of her smiling in the sunshine with bedhead, lips puffy from kissing. Beck's heart started to boom just looking at her. She appeared to still be half asleep as she turned onto her back, stretched her arms over her head and yawned. "You were telling me about community peach-picking day." Her voice came out sounding scratchy. "Why did you stop?"

Not touching her felt unnatural, so he reached across the bed and ran his fingers over her hip. "That was hours ago, darlin'. It's morning now."

"Oh." One eye popped open, followed by the other. "*Oh.*"

At her guarded tone, his mouth set itself in a grim line, hand dropping away from her warm skin. "You want to talk before or after breakfast?"

"There's a talk. I knew there'd be a talk." She sat up, propping herself against the headboard. "You don't waste any time."

The sight of her pointed nipples became too much for his sanity, so Beck stood and paced away from the bed. "I have to say my peace now, or I'll just climb back on top of you and forget my responsibilities. Forget everything but you."

She slid her hands over the sheets. An invitation. "Sounds like a plan."

Beck cursed, wishing for once that his body wasn't susceptible to every move she made. "I'm leaving tomorrow, Kenna."

Her beautiful face paled. "We always knew you were leaving."

"Is that your way of saying things haven't changed since day one?" The scar tissue on his right side started to throb. "Because you're going to need to be more convincing."

"What do you want me to say?" She shouted the words, then drew back, looking surprised at her own outburst. "I did as you asked. I didn't think about it last night, but last night is over. I don't know what you expect to happen next."

Beck shook his head, taking a measured step in her direction. "Last night might be over, but we're not." It hit him full force exactly what he had at stake here. His girl. The girl he wanted forever. So he'd fight and fight hard, just like he'd been taught. She was scared—he could see it in her wary expression—so he needed to be strong enough for both of them. "We have two options here, Kenna. You come with me back to Georgia. Or I stay here."

Her green eyes went wide. "*What?*" She gained her feet, taking the bedsheet along with her and wrapping it around her body like a protectant. "I-I can't...*you* can't—"

"I can. I will."

Just like their last morning together, he saw the bomb about to go off. Saw her frantically scanning the contents of her mind for something to distance him. Too bad it wouldn't work this time. He knew her now, knew her faults and insecurities and treasured each one individually. She could say any damn thing she chose and he would stand firm.

Beck saw the moment she realized it, too, because her features transformed with panic. "Maybe the only reason I hooked up with you was because it was temporary. Don't you think you're taking the whole morning afterglow thing a little too far?"

"No."

A beat of silence passed. "*No?* That's it?"

"Yeah." He advanced on her, catching her before she could trip over the sheet. "Here's what we're going to do now. We're going to knock off the bullshit. You understand?"

Kenna scoffed. "Yes, *Daddy.*"

She'd meant it to sound flippant, but his dick didn't think it was funny. Not after she'd been screaming the title just hours ago as he ate her pussy. Before he could explore his own mind, she was pinned to the wall, his jeans the only barrier between her heat and his erection. It relieved him to a startling degree when some of the fight left her, a small moan passing her lips. "You want daddy, you'll get me, but you'll hear me out and give me an answer first."

Her stubborn mouth snapped shut, eyes firing bullets at him.

"My body reacted to you first. I won't lie. But my heart followed a minute later and I was yours. Yours to *keep*. There is something good and strong between us, and I'm not giving it up." Her eyes softened slightly, forcing him to beat back the urge to kiss her and forget the argument. "I will take you to Georgia and give you a home. I'll make a place for you to build your statues. I will fuck you every night and love you as much as you can stand, Kenna Sutton."

When he finished his speech, her eyes were full of tears, but he knew with absolute certainty she wouldn't let a single one fall. It didn't bother him one bit, though. Her pride was one of the reasons he'd fallen for her.

"Beck." Her voice wavered. "I don't know how to belong to someone. I don't know how to have someone belong to *me*."

Her words flayed him alive, but he forced himself to step back, letting her slide down the wall. "I know what I'm asking. It's a leap of faith, and I won't force a decision out of you right now." Hating the distance he had to put between them, Beck backed toward the door. "I need you at the ceremony tonight. Can you give me that?"

She nodded vigorously, but her gaze was on the floor. "I'll be there."

Before he left the room, he stopped in the doorframe and waited for her attention. "Two choices, Kenna. Let me know which one it'll be. Tonight."

He left the apartment, praying like hell his gamble would pay off.

# CHAPTER ELEVEN

Kenna paced outside the packed auditorium. She had to be out of her damn mind coming here, dressed like some kind of teenage debutante. Her feet were light without combat boots to anchor them down, her body felt somehow more exposed than usual in the knee-length white lace dress. She tugged the secret flask from her purse and took a belt of whiskey, hoping it would calm her cartwheeling nerves, to no avail. Georgia. She was going to Georgia.

After Beck had left this morning, she sank into a hot bath and sat there until it went cold. Then she'd made spaghetti for breakfast and brought it in a bowl down to her workshop. About an hour had passed before she realized she hadn't picked up a single tool. Or taken a bite of the spaghetti. She'd been in shock. She could count on one hand the times she'd felt *wanted* or important in her life. Most of them had come in the last few years via Darla. Once or twice while her father had been recovering from the heart attack, he'd let her see his appreciation for her help. But being on the receiving end of Beck's proposition this morning had thrown her like a paper airplane into a tornado.

Snippets of their night together had started to trickle in once the shock wore off. Beck had called her *nurturing*. At the time, she'd found it ridiculous. Now, though? She wondered. Why had she stuck around Black Rock so long when—at age twenty-two—she was free to go anywhere? When she could move her business wherever she decided to live?

Was she waiting around, hoping her parents would need her? Hoping they would forget the past and include her in their new lives? The time she'd spent aiding her father's recovery had pulled her off the path of destruction she'd been intent on traveling, giving her a reason to shape up. But what if her apparent caretaker nature was doing more harm than good now? Every day that passed without word from her family felt like a physical blow, felt like being abandoned all over again for something better. Brighter.

It stopped now. What she felt for Beck was scary, especially after such a short space of time. It fluttered wildly in her stomach, begging her to climb over her mountain of fears and slide down the other side, right into his open arms. Yes, there was a part of her that wanted to heal Beck's wounds, soothe his soul. That newly admitted facet of her personality asked to be fostered. Beck recognized that part of her and accepted it, so long as her need for him ran beneath it, true and straight. And it did. She needed to be with him so badly, it sang in her ears like whistling wind.

*You're here to take the leap.* There would be no backing out now…and hell, she didn't want to. She couldn't wait to see Beck's face when she told him. Couldn't wait to be held against his chest, hear his heartbeat. Kenna popped a breath mint into her smiling mouth and clicked in silver high heels toward the auditorium entrance. When she opened the door, she heard Beck's deep voice coming from the stage and her heart carried her toward the sound she craved. She stopped just inside the back exit, pleasure settling in her middle at the sight of Beck in his dress blues, speaking from behind a podium. She'd never seen him in this capacity, commanding an entire room and yet, it didn't surprise her. Their eyes met and he stopped speaking, his throat working as he perused her from head to toe.

A man seated behind Beck on stage cleared his throat, obviously prompting the major to keep going, which he did a moment later. "It is with gratitude that I accept this Silver Star. Men who came before me—good, self-sacrificing men and women—have accepted this honor and I can only hope to live up to their legacies." His eyes found Kenna's, as if garnering strength. "But I'll be accepting it on behalf of Xander Gibbons, and I'd like this medal to go to his family. He wasn't the only soldier who gave his life that day so I could stand before you here, but he was one of the best men I've ever known and his name should be remembered."

Kenna caught Beck's subtle nod to a dark-haired officer standing off to the side. The man she'd seen with him at Bombs Away. Just as he'd been last night, the man appeared to be losing a brooding contest with himself. The lines of his handsome face were drawn taut and even across the distance his eyes looked bloodshot. She returned her attention to Beck just in time for respectful applause to break out and him to exit the stage. He stopped to clasp his friend's shoulder and say something before moving toward the double doors that led to the surrounding hallway, the same one where she stood, but he would be emerging around the corner and down a corridor. She started to back away from the crowd, intent on meeting Beck, but she saw him pause before leaving, watched his face register surprise.

To his friend's right stood a pretty blonde she hadn't noticed upon arriving, but the woman looked familiar, nonetheless. Too familiar. It only took Kenna a split second to remember the picture she'd seen in Beck's wallet. Mary. Beck's ex-girlfriend, Mary.

An invisible fist closed around her throat, cutting off her oxygen. Her legs began to shake with the urge to run as fast as she could. It would be over now. *Look at them.* They were a ten-year age progression of the homecoming king and queen. Stupid perfect. Mary had her hand on Beck's arm, big, bluebell eyes pleading, white teeth flashing as she whispered to him.

Kenna could feel the cool air from outside drifting in through the doorway behind her, enticing her to leave. Not yet, though. Once she saw it done, she could bail and bail hard. Audience members had started to take notice of the golden couple, watching them curiously, but Beck led Mary toward the exit, stifling the disruption.

Kenna drifted in their direction.

* * *

*Jesus, this couldn't be happening.*

He'd walked off the stage, raw from revisiting the tragedy that had taken Xander and wanting nothing more than to soak up comfort from Kenna. Seeing her appear in that doorway, dressed like an angel, had given him the strength to get through the acceptance speech. Her answer had been written on her face. Yes to Georgia. Yes to him. Yes to everything. The beating organ in his chest had swelled to the point of bursting, so full, so grateful.

Out of nowhere, Mary had appeared. Confusion had stopped him in his tracks, followed by a brief flash of nostalgia. Not because he had any lingering feelings for Mary. He hadn't for a long time and now…now he couldn't fit a single damn thing around what Kenna made him feel. No, Mary's appearance had made him think of the past. A time when things were simple and he didn't know what it felt like to lose a friend. Lose a battle. But she belonged in that time. The past. Not here and not now.

That's when panic had hit him. The glow on Kenna's face had dimmed and he could feel her slipping away bit by bit, all the way across the auditorium. Now he stood in the empty hallway, Mary crying and imploring him…for what? He couldn't hear her over the roaring in his ears. He needed to go after Kenna, but his feet were cemented to the ground. With absolute confidence, he knew if he turned the corner and saw she'd run away, he would break. Wouldn't be able to handle it. Not after having their future right there, in the palm of his hand. Her trust issues, her fear of being abandoned, couldn't handle this yet. With more time, he would have gotten her there, but it was too damn soon for this.

Mary gripped his arm and he wanted to jerk away. No one touched him but Kenna.

As if he'd called her name out loud, Kenna rounded the corner and stepped into view. The mere sight of her quieted the ceaseless wail of sound drowning everything else out, allowing him to focus. *My girl is so beautiful. So hurt when there's no reason.* Couldn't she see the gaping hole in his chest where she fit so perfectly?

*Focus.* He hadn't lost her yet. She was still there. The possessive beast inside him demanded he storm toward her, shake her and kiss her until she stopped looking so devastated. Her loss of hope was an insult to that ferocious part of him. Logic, however, managed to wedge its foot in the door. She needed time to reason this out. This moment was equally important to both of them. He needed her trust. She needed to learn how to give it.

"It's just...you were gone so long. I couldn't just wait around, getting older." Mary sobbed into the sleeve of her coat and Beck felt a pang of sympathy. He harbored no ill will for her. They'd been children with grown-up plans, and he didn't fault her for not wanting to put her life on hold for him. "But I know I messed up bad, Beck. When I heard you were coming back, I thought maybe we could have a second chance."

Beck didn't answer. Every ounce of his energy and attention focused on Kenna. *Come on. Remember what I promised you.* Did she think he'd said those words this morning on a whim?

Beck's reality shifted when Kenna took a step toward the side exit, her gaze bouncing back and forth between him and Mary. She placed a hand on the steel exit bar and his blood went cold. No. If she left now, he would never convince her of his intentions, the truth of his feelings. It would start a pattern and they'd never break free. The rush of sound in his ears started again—

Kenna dropped her hand from the door, saying something under her breath, and Beck's pulse heated back up, started to race. When their gazes met, he saw bravery there and wanted to shout at the ceiling. *Thank God.*

Arms locked at her sides, Kenna came closer, staying just out of his reach.

"Hey, Mary?"

His ex-girlfriend jolted at the sound of another female voice, although how she could have missed his rapt attention on Kenna baffled him. Couldn't everyone tell he was taken? The fact was so carved in stone it had to be stamped on every inch of his body.

Mary swiped a hand across her eyes, darting a look between Kenna and Beck. "Y-yes?"

"I, um." Kenna shifted in her heels. "You seem nice and all, which kind of blows. I was hoping you'd be evil, maybe wearing a coat made of puppies or something." She took a step toward Beck. "But I'm sorry. You're going to have to fight me for him."

For the first time in his life, he experienced what it felt like to be weak and strong, both at the same time. His limbs shook with the need to hold her, while his heart rumbled like an approaching locomotive, gaining power with each passing second. Kenna had already been his, but nothing would ever compare to hearing her make it official, despite her own fears. Nothing.

Mary gave a resigned laugh. "Looks like someone beat me to it." She wedged her purse beneath her arm. "I can't even say I'm the least bit surprised. I knew if it wasn't me, a good woman was going to snatch you up one day and never let go."

As Mary repeated the words Kenna had said to him their first night together, her mouth fell open. *That's right, darlin'. You're that good woman. And I'm the luckiest fucking guy on the planet.*

Neither one of them broke eye contact as Mary turned and left the building. Beck wasn't sure he'd look anywhere but at Kenna ever again.

"So, yeah. I'm fighting for you," she whispered. "And I'll go with you to Georgia on one condition."

"Which is?"

Her smile melted the remaining ice in his chest. "I drive."

"Thank Christ." Beck lunged forward to grip the sides of her face. "You don't *have* to fight for me, you crazy, gorgeous girl." His thumbs swept across her cheeks. "Neither of us has to fight. We won."

Her laugh sounded slightly incredulous. "I mean, I was really ready to throw *down,* though."

Beck shook his head, dying to get started on the next sixty years with this girl. "It's a good thing you held off," he murmured, watching her green eyes go smoky. Yeah, she knew what was coming. "You're going to need your energy."

She gasped as he dipped down, wrapped his arms behind her legs and threw her over his shoulder. She recovered in time to smack his ass as they strode through the double doors, out into the night. Together.

# HUNTLEY & CULLEN

SOPHIE JORDAN

# CHAPTER ONE

Getting piss drunk sounded like a fine idea.

Not only was Cullen having a shit week, but Huntley had decided to walk into Bombs Away in a skirt shorter than she'd ever worn. Maybe this was part of his punishment. If it wasn't for him, Xander wouldn't have been over there. Xander wouldn't be dead.

The flirty hem danced around a pair of gold-skinned thighs. The soft cotton tank she wore fit her snugly, hugging breasts that she usually hid under blousy tops and sweaters. He had a hard enough time keeping her firmly in the friend zone. This just added to his misery. He had two real friends in this world—Beck and Huntley. The fact that they happened to be brother and sister only added to the utter wrongness of his sudden surge of lust.

He tilted his head back and finished his bottle of beer, trying to tear his eyes off her. He didn't need this right now. He especially didn't need all these meatheads looking her over like she was something they wanted to sink their teeth into. *Stand down. Not your job to babysit her tonight. Her brother is here.*

Despite the voice of reason whispering inside of him, he was tempted to find a blanket and drape it over her.

With a small shake of his head, Cullen turned to glare at the shots lined up in front of him. He downed one in a swift motion, slamming the glass back on the bar.

"Huntley," her brother began. Better him than Cullen. He wasn't in the mood to talk right now. "I didn't expect you tonight." Beck paused awkwardly. Cullen grimaced. He might as well have told his sister to take a hike for the injured look to cross her face. "There's something I need to speak with Cullen about. Let's meet tomorrow."

Cullen's stomach bottomed out. He knew what Beck wanted to talk about. This conversation was long overdue.

"You can't tell me whatever it is, too?" The hurt in Huntley's voice was undeniable, and he pushed down the urge to assure her she could stay. Looking out for her was instinctive, but Beck was right. She didn't need to be here for this shit.

Cullen motioned for another round of shots. More drinks were poured and he downed his glass in one motion. Beck didn't touch his. "Had a feeling this wasn't just a friendly get-together." Cullen waved at Beck's glass. "You going to drink that?"

"I'm good, man," Beck replied.

Cullen downed it.

"I didn't realize we were getting drunk tonight." Huntley blinked those big blues of hers, staring at Cullen with a hint of disapproval. Clearly, she wasn't leaving. Not so surprising. She usually did what she wanted.

Cullen looked her up and down and felt a flash of irritation again. With an internal curse, he slammed back another shot and let the alcohol slide down his throat. *So not cool, man. Her brother is right here.*

Over the years, he'd kept dirty thoughts at bay when it came to Huntley. He rarely let himself appreciate the dark blonde hair that fell to the middle of her back. Or her curvy legs. Like nuns and cousins, she was off limits. "I didn't realize you needed to be consulted."

"Is that how you speak to my sister?" Beck inhaled. "We'll have this discussion later."

Huntley looked good tonight. There was no denying. Too good. Not that she wasn't pretty, but she was never a wear-makeup-every-day kind of girl. She was the fresh-faced farm-girl type. *You ever heard the one about the farmer's daughter…*

Beck shifted beside him again, and Cullen eyed him, guessing his injuries must be paining him. Just another side effect from the mission that had killed Xander. Hell, Beck could have died, too. Cullen should be grateful, he supposed, that Beck had made it out. And he was, except Xander was gone. He couldn't quite shake that even though it had been months now.

Cullen stared straight ahead, catching glimpses of his stony reflection in the mirror behind the bottles of liquor. Sullen Cullen. He knew that's what people called him, and he didn't care. Hell, ever since he was a kid people called him that. Other kids. Teachers. When you never stayed long in one place, you forgot how to smile and make friends. What was the point? By the time he got to know anyone, he'd be gone again.

Now, here at Black Rock, it wasn't his job to make

friends. His job was to train soldiers in explosive ordnance disposal so that they saved lives. Xander was one of the first he had pushed to enter the program. One of the first he trained. One of the few he'd let in. One of the few he called a friend.

And now he was dead.

"It's about Xander, isn't it? You finally gonna tell me what happened over there?" He gestured for another drink and watched as the bartender poured it. "When you called to tell us he wouldn't be coming home, I knew you were holding back. You're a shit liar, Beck. Out with it. How'd he die? What the hell happened over there?"

As much as Cullen dreaded it, he needed to finally hear it. He'd been waiting to hear this.

Beck lifted his massive chest on a heavy breath. "If I could keep this from you forever, I would, because there's no sense in both of us feeling guilty, Cullen. But it's going to come out in the casualty report this week and I want it to come from me."

Cullen remained very still. Even Huntley looked uneasy.

Beck sighed. "We were extracting a group of POWs. They'd been there a week, but we couldn't get close enough or get an accurate count…"

Cullen listened to the steady recounting, the scene flashing clearly in his mind speaking only when Beck paused. "Finish what you have to say," he ground out.

"He got it wrong. The explosive went off and half the tunnel caved in. Most of us were in an offshoot that remained standing." Huntley leaned against her brother. Beck wrapped an arm around her and looked at Cullen. "This isn't on you. No amount of training—"

Cullen shook his head. If it wasn't on him, whose fault was it? He was the one who persuaded Xander to go into EOD. The one who trained him. It was on him and no one else. His fist shot out, sending the shot glasses crashing behind the bar. *Bullshit.* He shoved back his chair and took off toward the bar exit.

He didn't need anyone to tell him how to feel. Not even Beck.

He just needed to be alone.

* * *

Huntley's boot heels clacked on pavement as she hurried out of the bar after Cullen. Of all nights to don a pair of heels, it had to be a night she was required to run.

Cullen's longer legs put him far ahead of her. She focused on his gray T-shirt and jeans as his lean body cut across the parking lot. *Sweet Jesus, these boots were murdering her feet.* "Cullen, wait!"

He continued like he hadn't heard her, striding a hard line through the parking lot and stopping beside his truck. She ran the last bit of distance, determined to catch up with him even if she broke an ankle in these death contraption boots.

"Cullen!" She was almost to him now. The soles of her new boots skidded across loose gravel and her arms flailed at her sides until she regained her balance.

He lifted bloodshot eyes to her, and she knew they were only partly red from alcohol. The news he'd just gotten had hit him hard. The guilt of Xander's death was etched into every line of his face.

He eyed her impatiently as she came to a clumsy,

breathless stop before him. "What, Huntley? I'm not really in the mood right now for this."

This. *Her.* Like she was the biggest pain in his ass. Is that how he saw her all these years? She thought he enjoyed hanging out with her. An itchy feeling swept up her neck and swarmed her face. Did he resent keeping an eye on her for Beck? God knew he could have been doing other things with his time.

Her gaze flicked from him to the keys in his hand and resolve hardened inside her. Fine. She was about to become an even bigger pain in his ass. This friendship went both ways. He took care of her. Now it was her turn to take care of him. She was an emergency room nurse. She handled people in all manner of conditions. This wouldn't be such a stretch for her. Except Cullen wasn't some stranger. *He happens to be someone you regularly imagine naked.*

"You're not driving," she announced, adopting the voice she used with wayward patients.

"I'll be fine. I only had a few—"

"You only had a few that *I* saw. You were drinking before I even showed up." She snatched the keys from his hand.

He growled. It was the only word to describe it. The sound made the tiny hairs at her nape prickle with awareness. With his tall, hard body, dark hair and molten chocolate eyes, he rocked sexy. She couldn't walk down the street beside him without women breaking their necks to look him over.

But right now this awareness was different. For the first time he looked at her with an intensity that made her feel like a woman. Not his friend. Not Beck's sister. She felt stripped bare and vulnerable, the sole object of his rapt concentration.

She was also pretty sure he wanted to strangle her.

A vein throbbed in his forehead. She'd seen him like this one time before. They'd been leaving Java Joe's and someone had left his dog in the car on one of the hottest days of summer. Cullen had marched back inside and confronted the asshole with a few choice words.

God, she really was messed up. He was pissed and glaring at her and it actually gave her a thrill. She had to stop this. Get a boyfriend. Get laid. Stop fixating on Cullen like he was some forbidden dessert.

He held out his hand. "Hand them over, sweetheart."

Her fingers tightened around the keys, the metal digging into the tender flesh of her palm. She wasn't about to hand over his keys. He made a grab for them, but she thrust her fist behind her back, yelping when he wrapped an arm around her waist and hauled her against him in one hard move that brought them nose to nose.

The heels of her boots lifted off the ground, her toes grazing earth. Her eyes bugged as she stared down at him. Blinking was impossible. His forearm felt rock solid around her. She was no lightweight. She was five feet eight, and it had been years since she felt comfortable in a bikini … hell, even a swimsuit. Her breasts pillowed against his chest, and heat scalded her face as her nipples hardened. *Please, please, don't let him notice that.*

The only way she had even tolerated being around him all these years was because he didn't know the lustful thoughts that swirled through her when she got within two inches of him. That would be too mortifying.

"I'm not in the mood to play, Huntley."

She shivered at the gravel in his voice and the sensation of his long body against hers.

This man was a warrior. He dealt in death. He played with bombs, for God's sake. Maybe she shouldn't challenge him. Maybe she should be scared. He was drunk. Pissed. Hurt. But she knew him. She knew he loved barbecue with a side of barbecue. She knew he mowed the single mom's yard across the street. She knew he lost his virginity on a beach in Panama on his sixteenth birthday to a girl three years his senior. She knew he loved baseball and secretly liked cats. She knew he couldn't stand for his feet to be touched, and he thought *Jeremiah Johnson* was the greatest movie ever made.

And she knew she couldn't let him drive in this condition.

"I'm not playing," she countered.

Pressed up against him like this she practically felt petite. They had touched often enough over the years but never like this. She fought to swallow against the tightness in her throat.

"Then stop fucking with me and give me the keys."

She gasped. He never used language like that with her. The dirty word shot a spike of heat right through her as she imagined just that. Fucking. *Fucking him.*

She moistened her lips and that heat spread deeper through her as his dark eyes followed the movement of her tongue.

"I'm not fucking with you." God, had she actually uttered that word? Her grandma just rolled over in her grave. "You've had too much to drink to get behind the wheel, and after what you just heard tonight I don't think you're in any condition—"

"You don't think I can drive a fucking truck?"

She flinched.

"I've driven in a lot worse conditions than this," he bit

out. "Drunk. With a concussion. I've even driven through a smoke-infested desert with gunfire all around me. I'm trained to handle worse situations than this. I'm *supposed* to know how to deal with this kind of shit."

She knew they weren't talking about him driving home tonight anymore. This was about Xander.

"Cullen," she said softly, her heart aching for him.

The lines of his handsome face twisted tightly. "No. Don't talk to me like I'm one of your patients, Nurse Collier. I don't want your pity." He stepped back, holding his hands up in defeat. "Fine. You can drive me home." He growled the words like he was just humoring her.

"Good." Unlocking his truck, she climbed behind the steering wheel and waited as he walked around and climbed in through the passenger door.

She buckled up, gratified to see he did the same and she didn't have to ask him to.

When she looked up again, it was to catch him staring at her. He looked her up and down. "Nice skirt. New?"

Her face heated. He'd noticed. She *had* dressed to attract tonight, deciding it wouldn't hurt to give her legs a shave and practice looking nice. Especially since she'd joined an online dating site and had her first coffee date scheduled for tomorrow.

"Yeah. Thanks."

He turned and stared out the windshield. "Sure about driving me home? Looked like you were getting your fair share of attention. Maybe Mr. Right was in there."

Was she so transparent? Mortification burned her cheeks and she regretted confiding in him that she had joined an online dating site. It was time to move forward with her life.

He'd expressed his concern, of course. Beck had appointed him her protector while he was gone, after all, and Cullen took the responsibility seriously. Like any other task or duty appointed to him. He'd shadowed her life these last few years—a tame existence that consisted of work, reading and channel-surfing.

"There will be other opportunities," she dismissed with a shrug. Now wasn't the time to divulge about tomorrow's coffee date. She was talking to a few other guys, too. All nice-looking, solid types. An accountant, a gym coach and a financial advisor. No baggage-ridden soldiers looking to nail everything in heels. No, these were men who were settled and grounded and looking for a relationship. In short, men *not* like Cullen. She figured that was healthy. No sense looking for someone like Cullen. She was only setting herself up for disappointment if she did that.

There was no one like him.

It was still early as they drove through town. Plenty of soldiers prowled the streets, looking for a little action to finish off the weekend. All except the one next to her. He stared silently out the window, arms crossed over his lean chest. She tried not to let her gaze stray to him, but it was difficult. His snug gray T-shirt strained against the cut lines of his torso. He propped one elbow on the doorframe, and the tattoo on his bicep peeked out beneath the edge of his sleeve.

"You're going to miss the turn," he pointed out.

She hit the break and flipped the turning signal, taking a right onto Cullen's street. He rented a house at the end of a quiet street that was only a few minutes from base.

She lived in a condo about ten minutes away at the edge of Black Rock, but it was only temporary. She wanted roots.

A place of her own. Hopefully a man of her own, too. A boyfriend. Someday a husband. She winced. At twenty-six, she hoped that someday would be soon.

She knew her family wanted her to return to Georgia, but she liked her job and the life she'd made here. Back home felt like a continuation of high school. The same faces. The same people doing pretty much the same thing, telling the same stories. Only now they were all getting married to one another and giving birth to mini versions of themselves.

Her life was good here, but she could admit to herself that it could be better if she had someone to share it with.

She had fallen into a deceptively comfortable routine with Cullen. Not a Sunday afternoon went by where he didn't track her down at the library and then walk her to Java Joe's after she checked out her books for the week. Sometimes they watched movies and ordered a pizza. He'd ask about her day and share funny stories about his trainees. He always kept it light. He never made what he did feel serious or dangerous even though she knew it was. Even though she treated his trainees often enough when one of them blew off a hand or busted an eardrum in training.

It wasn't a bad life, but she wanted more. *Needed* more.

She pulled up in front of the one-story red-brick house and parked beside Cullen's motorcycle. He'd left a porch light on and it bathed the hood of the truck in a yellow glow. She turned off the engine and climbed down, following Cullen to the door.

He turned to face her, hand extended, palm out. A sardonic smile played on his mouth. "Can I have my keys now? So I can unlock the door?"

She tossed the keys and he caught them in one hand.

With a smirk, he turned and unlocked the front door.

He'd been renting the place for four years but still hadn't done much with it, inside or out. No special landscaping. Just a yard he kept mowed. Stepping inside, there were only the bare essentials. It was the quintessential bachelor pad. Kitchen table, couch and TV. A single bedroom and guest room he used as an office—both equally sparse.

The place smelled like him. She inhaled. There it was. Clean laundry and his brand of soap—whatever that was.

He tossed the keys down on the table and moved for the fridge, helping himself to another beer. She looked away when she caught herself staring at his ass. God, that man could rock a pair of jeans.

When she looked back he had turned around again. She watched the tendons of his tanned throat work enticingly as he drank deep.

What was it with her? True, she'd always thought he was hot, but this was ridiculous. It was almost like some invisible switch on her libido had been flipped when she signed up on that dating site.

"Guess you're stuck here now. Too bad for you. I'm shit company right now," he said, lowering the bottle from his mouth. He waved to the fridge. "Want one?"

"No, thanks."

"Course not." He took a long sip, his dark eyes surveying her.

"What's that supposed to mean?" She shifted where she stood. Right now dipping her feet in acid would have felt better than enduring another moment in these boots.

This time when he lifted the bottle from his mouth those well-carved lips curled in a smile that made her stomach flip. Damn, she hated that he had this effect on her. Mostly because it meant she was like every other girl and not immune to him. She didn't *want* to be like every other girl. She wasn't. She was different. For starters, she was his friend. The women traipsing in and out of his bedroom could never claim that. That should be enough. It should more than satisfy her.

"You're a lightweight. One of those girls who can't stand the taste of beer and drank Strawberry Hill all through high school. You probably never even got drunk back then. Just took your five sips of Hill and faked a buzz."

Crossing her arms, she glared at him even though he was closer to the truth than she liked to admit.

He chuckled as though he read her mind. "I'm right, aren't I, sweetheart? I can see you now in some farmer's field. Giggling and acting drunk. Probably letting some guy cop a feel and blaming it on the booze."

She sucked in a sharp breath. There was an edge of insult to his words. He *never* talked to her like this. It pissed her off until she remembered what he was going through. This wasn't about her. There was a reason he was pounding drinks like there was no tomorrow.

She moved to the table and plopped down on a chair. "It's okay," she announced as she tugged off one of her boots.

He frowned. "What's okay?"

"You can be nasty. I'll be your whipping dog if it makes you feel better. I know you don't mean it, and I know you're hurting."

His dark eyes flashed and he pushed off the counter, his knuckles whitening where they clutched the neck of his bottle. "Bullshit."

Maybe she shouldn't push him, but he needed a friend. Someone who didn't hold any punches and spoke honestly to him. Someone he couldn't intimidate.

"Cullen, you need to talk about it," she said gently.

He pointed an accusing finger at her. "Don't get all shrink on me, Huntley."

She yanked off her second boot and dropped it on the floor. "There's no shame in how you're feeling. You're entitled to feel bad. You can even take a night and get hammered."

"Is that right?"

She nodded. "Yeah. Grieve, cry ... but eventually you're going to have to talk about it—"

He cursed and tossed the empty bottle in the trash. "You want me to talk? You want me to tell you how I pushed Xander into the program, and when he had misgivings, I encouraged him to stick with it."

She winced. "That's your job. To train and support and encourage—"

"Yeah, well, I should have been more objective. I should have seen that he didn't have what it took."

"You don't know that," she protested, her heart aching for him. "It could have happened to anyone." She hated that he blamed himself. She knew how much he cared for his trainees. He gave everything, making sure they were prepared for the realities of what they were going to face over there.

"But it happened to him. One of my guys," he said flatly. He turned, removed another beer out of the fridge and disappeared into the bedroom.

She stared at her discarded boots, wondering what to do. It wasn't as though she could get in her car and drive away. She needed to call a cab or her brother or just accept she was staying the night, which really wouldn't be a big deal. It wouldn't be the first time they crashed under the same roof.

And there was the not-so-minor fact that she didn't want to leave him alone when he was like this.

After a moment, she rose and followed Cullen, stopping in the threshold of his room.

Her heart constricted at the sight of him in front of his closet. The muscles and sinew of his back rippled as he pulled his shirt over his head and dropped it to the floor. Her mouth dried as she focused on the line of his spine, the way it dipped and disappeared into the waistband of his jeans.

He turned, blasting her with his bare chest. The washboard abs, the happy trail that beckoned questing fingers. His hands moved, stopping at the button of his fly.

Her lips parted on a breath.

"Like the show?" He cocked a dark eyebrow and hesitated only a moment before shrugging and sliding his jeans down his narrow hips. He wore boxer briefs, and her ovaries kicked to life at the sight of the impressive bulge there. *Dear God, how big would that thing be fully aroused?*

He was beautiful. Toned and carved from marble. His skin was tanned, hinting at some Mediterranean lineage. The saliva rushed back into her mouth. She wanted to kiss and lick and bite every inch of his body. One of her dates better pan out soon because she couldn't keep eyeballing Cullen like this.

She shook her head. "Stop being so arrogant."

"It's who I am. You know that." He winked at her as he flipped on the TV and moved to pull back the covers.

"What are you doing?

"I'm going to watch TV and finish this beer until I pass out," he replied evenly as he slid beneath the dark blue sheets.

"Oh," she said dumbly.

"What about you? Gonna stay here and babysit me? Or call Beck to come get you?" He lifted his beer to his lips.

She didn't want to bother Beck. She told him she could handle Cullen. He would be leaving for home in a couple days, anyway. She didn't want him to worry that he was leaving behind a hot mess. He'd waited so long to return home. He loved the farm and was eager to get back to it. He was like their grandfather. The land was in his blood.

Cullen flipped to a rerun of the *The Big Bang Theory*. He patted the bed beside him. "Come on, sweetheart. You like this show."

Somewhat mollified at his familiar cajoling tone, she nodded. "I'll stay."

He pointed to his dresser. "You can change into one of my shirts."

"Thanks."

She moved and opened a random drawer, hearing him call out too late. "Wait. Not that drawer."

Her breath caught as her gaze fell on a pair of handcuffs. She looped a finger inside one of the steel circles and lifted it, turning as she asked, "Er, what are—"

He was standing right behind her now, staring steadily at her face, that naked chest of his radiating heat. "Those are mine. You know, for when I have friends over."

"Friends," she squeaked, "who like to be handcuffed?"

He rubbed a hand up and down the back of his scalp. "Well. Yeah. Among other things."

Her stomach pitched and came alive with flutters as she imagined what those *other* things could be. Her chest suddenly felt like a hundred-pound boulder sat on it. Try as she might, she could not draw enough air. She looked at the handcuffs and back to him again.

He shrugged like it was no big deal.

She moistened her lips, her interest piqued. "What … *other* things … do you do?"

He laughed and the sound curled through her belly in ribbons of heat. "Come on. You don't really want to know about this kind of thing."

She swallowed. "I do. I want to know."

His smile faded. He gazed at her for one long moment before shrugging again. "All right. Sometimes it gets a little rough."

"Rough?"

He nodded, clarifying. "Sex."

"Sex." God, she was a parrot now. She squared her shoulders and tried to convey she was a mature woman who could handle a discussion about sex. *Not just any sex. Sex the way Cullen did it.*

"Yeah. You know, a little spanking. Handcuffs on the headboard. That kind of thing."

Her eyes widened.

"Don't look so scandalized. I don't do whips or canes or anything. Nothing like that. I know it's not your cup of tea, but plenty of women get off on—"

"How do you know it's not my thing?" Her chin shot up.

He laughed and shook his head. "C'mon, sweetheart. I know you."

"You don't know *everything* about me."

"Right. Rough sex is your thing."

"Maybe."

He snorted. "Your face is the color of a tomato right now."

"S-so," she sputtered, hating that he thought he had her so figured out. Even if maybe he did. "You don't know what I would or wouldn't do in bed. Do you?" *God, just stop. Say nothing more.* "I mean, maybe I like that kind of thing, too." Great. Babbling and lying now.

Amusement danced in his dark eyes, but thankfully he didn't laugh. She couldn't have handled him laughing outright in her face.

"I guess I don't know," he allowed. "It's just you aren't exactly what I would call experienced—"

Her expression must have showed how much that statement felt like a jab. He quickly amended, "Hey, I just wouldn't think you were into anything more adventurous than—"

"Missionary?" She shot back. "Well, you aren't exactly versed in what I like when it comes to sex, are you?"

He gave her an unreadable look. "No. I guess I'm not."

Plucking the cuffs from her hands, he stuck them back inside the drawer and opened another one, his movements brisk and efficient. Taking out a T-shirt, he handed it to her. "Here you go."

She continued staring at him, those flutters still dancing in her stomach. "Thanks."

Turning, she shut herself inside the bathroom and changed into a soft cotton T-shirt that smelled like him. Even though the hem fell mid-thigh, she kept her skirt on since it fell a little lower. Stepping out of the bathroom, she found him back in bed again.

She settled down beside him, on top of the covers, telling herself this was no different than any other night they watched TV together on her couch. Even if she kept hearing

Cullen's deep voice in her head. *Sometimes it gets a little rough.*

Her sex ached and clenched, and she pressed her thighs together. His admission had done more than pique her curiosity. She couldn't shut off the idea of Cullen … and her … and rough sex.

So what if they were in his bed and she was aroused *and* she had shaved her legs? He wasn't going to make a move, and she sure as hell wouldn't. Even if she wanted to, it would take more courage than she possessed to make the first move. That kind of forwardness wasn't in her DNA.

She held herself rigidly beside him through two episodes. The tension didn't ebb from her body. Her skin felt itchy and tight. Even if she hadn't already seen these shows, she wouldn't have been able to focus on the actors. Out of the corner of her eye, she watched the rise and fall of his hard chest, the slope of his ridged stomach. The glint of his dog tags above his sternum.

This was insane. Her body was primed and ready to go. It had been four years since she slept with a guy. Since sex. Four years since Jackson broke up with her. Since then, there had only been the occasional kiss on a rare date. Maybe a little fondling over clothes. Her body was a drought and right now Cullen the long-withheld water. She swallowed and scratched at her itchy skin. She couldn't handle the proximity to him.

She shifted her weight, scooting to the edge of the mattress, as far as she could go without falling. She was never going to relax, and she was stuck here for the entire night. Sleep was impossible.

That was her persistent and final thought, the last she would remember before falling asleep.

# CHAPTER TWO

Huntley was asleep.

In his bed.

It was a hell of a situation, and he could not quite wrap his mind around it. The one woman he would never fool around with was in his bed, curled up on her side with her back to him, her skirt riding high enough for him to glimpse her white cotton panties. White cotton panties that shouldn't have been hot, but for some reason they got him as stiff as a pike. His palms itched to grip the flesh, to discover if her ass felt as firm as it looked.

He cursed and flipped to the History Channel. A war movie was playing. He grimaced. The last thing he wanted to watch, but it might cool his ardor. After thirty seconds of explosions, he cursed and flipped to Comedy Central.

The comedian only held his attention for so long before his gaze strayed to Huntley again. He tapped the remote control anxiously against his leg and eyed the length of her smooth thighs on display. The swell of her ass pushed against the white cotton of her underwear.

She normally wore jeans and bulky sweaters. Blouses when the weather was warmer. He'd never seen so much of her body on display. Never had a clear idea of her shape before. He knew she was tall. Not thin. Not fat. She had always simply been Huntley.

Right now, she reminded him of those pinup girls from the 1940s. Juicy curves. Soft swells and dips and hollows that screamed femininity. He adjusted his cock, hoping to ease the throb there. No relief. Instead, he gave himself a few strokes as he stared at the long stretch of her legs and the two dimples on her lower back, directly above the top of her panties.

"Fuck," he muttered. Getting a hard-on for his best friend's sister could not be happening. Beck trusted him. He expected him to treat her with respect. She wasn't some hook-up.

He should have brought someone home from the bar tonight. A regular at Bombs Away who he'd fucked before who knew how to play the game. It would have been one way to get his mind off Xander, and Huntley wouldn't have insisted on following him home. He wouldn't be so cock-hungry for her right now.

Flinging back the covers, he picked up his beer bottle from his nightstand. He deposited it in the trash and shut off all the lights in the house. Moving to his bathroom, he brushed his teeth before flattening his hands on the counter and staring at himself in the mirror.

He never should never have recruited Xander. If he hadn't, the guy would still be alive. His bloodshot eyes stared daggers back at him. He scrubbed both hands over his face and tried to push back the urge to shout or hit something.

Beck's words played over and over in his head. *He got it wrong. He got it wrong.*

Cullen had trained him. Xander wasn't supposed to get it wrong over there. Maybe Cullen was the one who got it wrong. Maybe he left something out, some key point of instruction. It wouldn't be the first time he made a bad call. According to his father, he only ever made bad calls. Going into EOD instead of intelligence was his worst. He was twenty-nine years old, but his old man never missed a chance to remind him that he was a total disappointment.

With a disgusted snort, he flipped off the bathroom light and then the TV as he passed it on the way to bed. The room was shrouded in shadows, the only light creeping in from the blind slats. The neighbor had left their back porch light on and a low glow suffused his bedroom, outlining the furniture.

He slipped into bed and turned on his side. Huntley had rolled onto her back, and he watched her chest rise and fall with breaths. She was still stretched out on top of the covers.

Sitting up on one elbow, he lifted her slightly, tugging the comforter all the way down. His nose brushed her hair and he inhaled the fruity scent. Some kind of melon maybe? Strawberry? He resisted the impulse to bury his nose in her hair. "Shit," he laughed lightly, without mirth. "You need to lay off the booze, man."

For no other reason could he fathom his response to Huntley. They'd been hanging out for years. Never had he inhaled her hair or entertained salacious thoughts of her ass.

Even if she wasn't Beck's sister, she still wasn't his type. She was a good girl. She wanted marriage, white picket fences and a passel of kids. And she wanted it yesterday. For God's sake, she joined an online dating service. He hadn't missed that gleam of interest in her eyes as he explained his sexual preferences, but he would forget it. He had to. He wouldn't ruin her.

He lowered her back down, tugging the covers over her. She sighed softly against his throat and his skin reacted, tightening almost painfully. He quickly released her.

Dropping back on his pillow, he made certain a good foot separated them. Flinging an arm across his forehead, he gazed up at the ceiling where his thoughts found their way back to Xander. The pain was still there, slicing through him. Guilt so deep he felt like he was drowning in it. His fault. His failure. His father always said he had no business in EOD. It wasn't a Thanksgiving without that reminder. *You have no business in EOD. It takes nerve and guts. You lack both, boy.*

His chest squeezed and his hands opened and closed like he was seeking something to grab, something to pull him free from the quagmire.

*Someone.*

His gaze slid left to Huntley again and he laughed once, a low, tormented sound. He really was one broken SOB.

His friend was dead because of him, and he was in bed with a hard-on for his other friend's sister. This might be the lowest point in his life. Considering his less-than-stellar upbringing, that was saying something.

He expelled a breath and returned his gaze to stare blindly at the ceiling again. Gradually, his eyes grew heavy. The alcohol chugging through his system was finally working its magic. With a heavy exhale, he closed his eyes.

# CHAPTER THREE

Huntley woke to a darkened room. She blinked sleepily against the murky light and struggled for a moment to remember where she was. She sniffed, missing the usual sugar-and-vanilla aroma of her condo. It probably didn't help her near-insatiable longing for cookies, but the aromatic candles comforted her and made her remember her grandmother's kitchen.

This space smelled musky. There was a bare hint of leather and laundry detergent and … soap. Man. *Cullen.*

Awareness flooded her. The events of the night rushed back. Bombs Away with her brother and Cullen. Driving Cullen home. Getting into bed with Cullen.

*In bed with Cullen.*

Panic and something else that felt dangerously close to excitement sizzled through her. She was on her side under the blankets—somehow she ended up underneath. She could feel the heat of Cullen radiating at her back. He drew her like a warm fire, beckoning her to come out of the cold.

She closed her eyes. It had been so long, and she had rarely ever spent the night with Jackson. Sex with him had been hasty trysts in the back of his car or at one of their houses while their parents weren't home. There was never a lot of privacy and always a sense of urgency.

She had lived at home while completing her nursing degree, and he had never moved out of his parents' home after high school. He was following in his dad's footsteps and planned to take over the family hardware store. Sleeping in a bed with a man was a whole new experience for her, and her stomach felt like it was alive with a thousand butterflies. And not just any man. Cullen. Sexy, hard-body, dark-eyed Cullen. *Sometimes it gets a little rough.* God. She would never get his voice, those words, out of her head.

She shifted slightly and became aware that her skirt was around her hips. Her legs slid sinuously against the sheets. She lifted her head and dared a peek behind her at the still, long line of his body. The curve of his muscled shoulder. The shadowed angles of his face looked slightly softer in sleep. He was on his side, too; his bigger body limned in the pale glow of light seeping from the blinds. If she just snuggled back one more inch they would be spooning.

His soft breath fell with the even cadence of sleep. What would it hurt? He was asleep. For just a moment she could experience what it felt like to share a bed with a man. A man and not a boy who spent all his free time playing video games.

She inched back until the warm wall of his chest was flush with her back. She aligned her bent legs against his so they fit together like two snug spoons.

Air shuddered from her lips at the simple contact, at

this closeness. She found herself regretting that she wore a shirt and could not feel the ridged contours of his chest and stomach without the barrier of clothing. Man to woman. Flesh to flesh. She yearned for it. For *him.*

His mouth was directly in her hair, his warm breath fanning the strands. The heat from his crotch scalded her bottom. She pushed back, ever so slightly, settling against that part of him. Curiosity emboldened her. She could feel the ridge of him there. Only the thin barrier of her panties and his briefs separated them.

It was terrible of her, but she wiggled. She couldn't stop herself. Her breath quickened as she felt him grow. It was awful what she was doing—using him for her own cheap thrills while he slept—but desire seethed through her. Her sex pulsed, clenching with need. It had been too long. The vibrator in her bedside drawer couldn't get her off like this.

She bit her lip and swallowed back a whimper as she rubbed her bottom against him. It was a mistake. Even if taking advantage of Cullen while he slept wasn't wrong, now she ached with desire.

She couldn't handle another moment of this self-inflicted torture. She would sleep the rest of the night on his couch. Live and learn. She flung the covers back and started to ease away.

She had one foot on the floor when a hand grabbed a fistful of her shirt and hauled her down on the bed. Her back hit the mattress with a soft thud. A woosh of air escaped her as Cullen loomed over her, larger than life, his shoulders rock solid and bunched with tension that undulated down to his taut biceps.

His hands flattened against the mattress on either side of

her shoulders, his arms twin bands of muscle that effectively caged her in. Her stomach dipped and twisted at the sight of so much masculinity hovering on top of her.

She moistened her lips as she looked up into his shadowed face. His short hair hugged his scalp, accentuating his carved features. That face was like a damned Calvin Klein model. Hard lines and chiseled good looks. The throb at her core pulsed deeper.

She felt herself drowning in the liquid depths of his eyes. They devoured her, gleaming like pools of dark water. This was unknown territory. She had seen Cullen in action with other women. She knew that he could be intense and almost predatory, but she had never thought he would direct all that intensity on her.

He must be confused. Or still drunk. Yeah, that made sense. More sense than him looking at her like she was his next meal. That made zero sense.

"Cullen?" Her voice escaped in an embarrassing croak. She tried again, telling herself that this wasn't weird. This was Cullen. Her friend. "Are you … drunk?"

"I'm sober enough."

If he wasn't drunk, then that meant she woke him up with her shameless bump and grind. Nice. That was only slightly mortifying.

The air crackled between them as she searched for words to explain herself. Maybe he hadn't noticed what she was doing before she tried to slip out of bed. A girl could hope.

His gaze dipped, moving down the length of her. She became hyper-conscious of the cool air wafting around her exposed thighs. She didn't need to glance down to know her flirty little skirt was sky-high to her hips and he had a view of her plain underwear. She flushed hotly. So boring. He was probably used to animal-print G-strings.

"You're not going to run out of here and pretend you didn't just back that ass into me."

His voice was a growl and almost unrecognizable to her. This wasn't her friend. It was a different Cullen.

A sound escaped her that sounded a lot like *omiphhhfttt*.

His gaze dipped again. He angled his head, studying her as though she were a specimen he had never seen.

Before she knew his intention, his hand came down and molded to her sex. She cried out at the contact. The firm press of his palm, the long fingers curling inward between her thighs, made her jump. His hand burrowed, gliding along the crease of her womanhood.

She whimpered, her hands stretching out at her sides and clutching the sheets. She parted her thighs in welcome, allowing him greater access and loathing the thin cotton barrier of her panties. His fingers rubbed, sliding against her until the friction became unbearable. She pushed herself against his fingers, hungry and seeking. His attention shifted back and forth from between her legs to her face, his expression fierce and concentrated.

That look should have frightened her, but she only wanted his fingers pressing deeper. She wanted her panties gone and his touch directly on her flesh, stroking her. Penetrating her.

Her eyes drifted shut at the near pain of her need.

"Open your eyes," he commanded, his voice thick and hard.

Her eyes snapped open and her gaze settled on him.

"Do you like this?" he demanded, continuing his

assault, rubbing his fingers against the crotch of her panties until she was soaking wet. His jaw was locked tight, his eyes hard obsidian.

She nodded, her hair tossing all around her.

"Say it. Tell me."

"Y-yes. I like it."

"What do you want, Huntley?" He twisted his wrist, pushing down against her clit with the base of his palm.

"This … harder … more." Ever since she saw those handcuffs, she had been one aching ball of need.

A corner of his mouth curled upward in a look that could only be described as supreme satisfaction. Instead of giving her what she asked for though, he lifted his hand away. She cried out, leaning forward at the loss of his touch.

He settled his knees between her legs and shoved her back down with one hand on her shoulder. His face was closer now. Directly above her. Even in the gloom of the room she could make out the brackets on either side of his mouth.

She held her breath, waiting, knowing something was coming even if she didn't know what. It occurred to her then that nothing with Cullen would be ordinary or expected. Even if her experience in the bedroom wasn't so limited, he was a man out of her realm.

She parted her lips, moistening them with her tongue. His eyes followed the movement and seemed to gleam darkly bright. *He's going to kiss me now.* He inched forth just a fraction, his mouth getting closer—

His fingers slapped her between the legs, coming down with a quick pat on her swollen sex.

A shudder wracked her and she moaned.

"You like that?" he asked against her ear.

She nodded and cried out as he swatted her sex again. The contact sent a bolt of sensation to her engorged clit.

"I warned you I was shit company, didn't I?"

She nodded, incoherent sounds breaking loose from her throat.

"You shouldn't be here, Huntley." This time he targeted her clit, striking her with a series of flicks that shot sharp needles of desire straight through her.

She cried out, shaking. She was so close.

His big hands dove to her hips. He grabbed the sides of her underwear and slid them down her legs in one move. Cool air wafted over her weeping sex.

She felt his stare there, on her swollen center. He saw the evidence of what he did to her … how wet she was, how she ached for him.

A hissed breath of approval escaped him. "Huntley." His voice sounded strangled. He placed a hand on the inside of each of her thighs, pushing her wide for him. "God, you're so pretty."

She'd never been so exposed in her life. Jackson never looked at her there.

Cullen lowered himself so she could feel his hot breath on her folds. "So fucking pretty, Huntley. Who knew you had such a sweet little pussy?"

Her breath fell in hard pants. She trembled, feeling his gaze like a touch and yet not. It wasn't a caress, and she needed it to be. She needed it so, *so* badly.

He dragged a finger down her, barrier free, tracing her slit. She surged off the bed, her spine curving at this first contact. A rush of moisture rose to meet him, and he made a tsking sound of approval.

With the same finger, he found her clit and circled it softly. She writhed on the bed, dying as he teased and rolled that tight bundle of nerves.

"Cullen," she begged.

"You're going to have to say it, Huntley."

She should have noticed something was off in his voice. That this wasn't just hot-and-bothered Cullen, but Cullen on the edge of something dangerous. But she was too lost to the dark desire pumping through her to process. "Say w-what?"

"Say it," he commanded, still stroking, but not exerting nearly enough pressure for her.

"H-harder."

"Harder … what, Huntley?"

"Push harder!"

"Like this?" He pressed down, rolling the clit and then easing off again, treating her only to the softest touch.

She whimpered and bucked against his hand. He was deliberately denying her and it was killing her. That mouth of his kicked up at the corner again.

She growled in frustration and he chuckled lightly, the sound curling through her. "You're going to have to talk. Tell me what you want, Huntley. Then maybe I'll give you the mouth-fuck you want."

She moaned. "You're torturing me."

He settled his hands on either side of her thighs and loomed over her like a hungry beast, the sinews in his arms and shoulders flexing. His gaze tracked down her body to her thighs before shooting back up to her face. "We're just getting started."

His hands circled her ankles and yanked her back down

on the mattress, sending her skirt up to her hips again. The roughness of the move, his quickness in which his big hands slid up from her ankles to her thighs, should have alarmed her. Instead, a hot thrill chugged through her veins. His strength and power and intensity excited her.

His face lowered between her thighs, his hands splaying her wide open for him. A moan spilled from her when his mouth latched onto her clit with single-minded precision. Her arms stretched out at her sides, seeking a handhold and fisting in his sheets. *Ohmygodohmygod!* She arched as he devoured her like she was his last meal.

He sucked her clit into his warm mouth, laving the sensitive bud, lapping it furiously, flaying her with his tongue. When his teeth scraped the button, her body shuddered. Her hands flew off the bed, grabbing his head, fingers delving into his cropped hair.

"Cullen!" She tugged on his head "What are you doing?" She didn't know what was happening. She felt like she was coming apart at the seams.

"I'm making you come," he purred against her sex. "No boy ever made this pussy tremble?"

She clutched his scalp, whimpering as his mouth found the entrance to her sex. He thrust his tongue inside. It only added to the torment. She needed him there. She cried out, bucking against his lips, begging for as much.

He lifted his face on a growl.

He crawled back up her body like a stalking predator, snatching both her wrists and pinning them to either side of her head. She lost herself in his dark gaze as his hard body flattened against her, his muscled arms stretched above her, holding her in place, his chest flat over hers, crushing her breasts.

"I'm going to make you come, Huntley." His rock-hard erection settled against her throbbing core.

She gasped at the sensation. Even with his briefs on, she could make out the huge ridge of him. It felt impossible, like it couldn't possibly fit.

But she hungered for it. Wanted it. Her legs lifted of their own volition and wrapped around his waist, welcoming him in. She began rocking and grinding against his cock in a simulation of sex.

"God," he gasped, dropping his mouth to the crook of her neck. "You're begging for a hard fuck. How long has it been?"

"Too long," she choked.

Was this it? Would her secret fantasy become a reality? Were they going to forget all the reasons why this couldn't happen? She shook her head on the bed, lifting her hips. *Please. Yes.* It felt surreal. As though this were merely another fantasy and not something playing out in actuality.

She rotated her hips, moaning at the rub of his erection against that part of her where all sensation centered. This couldn't only be to punish her. His cock was hard. He wanted her, too.

His briefs were damp from her, and she felt the head of him prod, so big and hard at her entrance. She thrust into him with a whimper, working her hips, hating that barrier, wishing it gone.

"God," he gasped, thrusting and pushing his enormous erection into her, pinning her hands deeper into the mattress. "You want me naked, don't you? I could be in you so fast, so deep. That'd finish you off, wouldn't it?"

"Yes," she choked, pleaded. That was what she wanted. He could do it. Take her. Fuck her. She couldn't even think of anything else she wanted more.

"More," she gasped, desperate for the pressure, something, anything, even the pop of his fingers against her over-sensitized nerves again.

She arched her spine, on the verge of tears. She still needed more. She lifted a hand, reaching for him, hoping to entice him inside her but he grabbed her hands and pushed them back on the mattress.

She gasped in pleasure at the feel of his heavy weight pressing her down on the bed. Her core was beneath his hard stomach. She would have preferred to feel his cock against her, but he didn't seem willing to give her that.

"You don't touch," he commanded in a voice that sent shivers through her. She felt dominated and possessed in a way she never knew she even craved.

He released one of her wrists and slid a hand between them. Dark eyes fastened to her face, he ran a single finger against her wet folds.

She was making all kinds of embarrassing sounds now, lifting her hips for his questing fingers.

He impaled her with a finger, penetrating deep and curling his middle finger slightly inside her, hitting that place she never quite managed to reach on her own.

The shudders started again, working up from her toes, traveling to her core and out from every limb. She was close. So close. He withdrew that finger and plunged it back in again. "You're so fucking tight, Huntley." His thumb found her clit and he bore down on it as he worked a second finger inside her.

"Oh!" Everything squeezed tight and twisted, bursting into a thousand pinpricks of sensation as he stroked deep inside her, wringing out a shrieking orgasm from her body. Her vision grayed at the edges. She fisted the sheet as her climax ripped through her. She gasped, trying to recover her breath as she dropped back on the bed. She pressed a palm to her cheek, fighting to steady her racing pulse. Impossible.

Emotion surged through her and she wasn't certain where it was coming from. Tears blurred her eyes and she blinked fiercely. With her freed hand, she lowered it to his bare shoulder, the muscled flesh slick and flexing under her palm.

Her body gradually floated back down, her pulse steadying.

*Oh. My. God. What just happened?*

She lifted her chin. Her gaze collided with Cullen's. He still looked intense and fierce and a little frightening. She shifted slightly beneath him and felt his raging hard-on, still there, still very much unsatisfied against the inside of her thigh.

"Cullen..." She moistened her lips, unsure of herself.

Something flickered in his eyes. She held her breath, waiting for him to speak. To assure her that he was glad this had happened. That this was not the worst thing to happen to him in the history of ever. That he had wanted it.

That he wanted her.

He looked at her beneath him as if seeing her for the first time and blinked once. "Shit."

With that curse, he sprang off her and dropped to the floor in one deft move.

She inhaled a shaky breath. Okay. That hurt. But at least

she knew where things stood. She shoved her skirt down and scooted to the edge of the bed, scanning for her panties and trying not to show how much his rejection stung.

"Huntley, listen—"

"No." She whirled around and faced him with the bed between them. "There's nothing to say. Forget it."

Before he could add anything else, or worse, before she broke down and started crying, she rushed out into living room, grabbed her bag and ducked into the hall bathroom.

Flipping on the light, she stared at her reflection in the harsh fluorescent glare. Her eyes looked overly bright and huge in her face. Her skin was flushed. Even her lips looked redder, puffier. She realized with a start that he had not even kissed her. Well, he hadn't kissed her on the mouth. She traced her lips with fingers that trembled the barest amount.

Her sex tingled and clenched, ready for round two. Or ready for the real thing. Him between her legs. Pumping inside her. Claiming her.

She groaned and dropped her head. This was too mortifying. Clearly, he was horrified things had gotten so out of hand. She had to end this and get things back into proper perspective between them. They were friends. Good friends. He was her brother's best friend.

Resolve squared her shoulders. She reached inside her bag for her phone. After a quick search, she dialed for a cab to pick her up. Hanging up, she slipped her underwear back on and ran fingers through her wild hair, wondering how long she could hide in the bathroom. She stared at the paneled wood. It wasn't exactly like he was knocking on the door. He'd probably be relieved to see her go.

# CHAPTER FOUR

Usually women didn't dive into bathrooms after making out with him. Not that Cullen usually made out with women. He wasn't seventeen. When he was with a woman, the outcome was sex. Pure and simple. They were both in it for the same thing, and that expectation was clear on both sides going in.

Tonight though, with Huntley, had been something else. Something organic. Something wild and unprecedented for him.

And they hadn't even had sex. A fact that both tormented and relieved him. On one hand he wanted her so badly his teeth ached. On the other hand, there was still time to salvage their friendship.

Huntley had been in the bathroom for ten minutes before she emerged. She paused when she saw him sitting on the couch. He'd thrown on a T-shirt and jeans. Partly to make her feel more comfortable, but mostly in case his dick decided to misbehave again and rise to full-mast.

To say he was sexually frustrated would be an

understatement. Seeing her again only drove home how much he wanted her. She looked well-pleasured. Her face flushed and her eyes shining.

"Hey," she murmured, flags of color staining her cheeks. "I called a cab."

Those words doused him in cold. "What did you do that for?"

"I don't think I should stay the rest of the night, do you?"

"I can sleep on the couch."

She shifted on her bare feet, looking uncomfortable. "I want to go home."

"So I'll take you home. I'm sober enough now."

She arched an eyebrow. "You sure about that?"

"What's that supposed to mean?"

"A sober Cullen never would have—"

He laughed roughly. "Oh, you're going to blame what happened on the alcohol?" He snorted, draping his wrists over his knees. "That's original, Huntley. The beer lowered my inhibitions? Really? I wouldn't have touched you otherwise?" He rubbed at his lips, tasting her there. "You go ahead and tell yourself that if it makes you feel better."

Her chest lifted on a sharp inhale, her full breasts pressing against the cotton of her blouse, and he suddenly regretted that he had not gotten her naked while he had the chance. He could have satisfied his curiosity after all these years.

It had always been there, buried beneath the surface. Sure, he treated her like she was one of the guys. Just another pal. It was the only way a friendship between them could work. But tonight he had crossed the line. It wasn't irreparable, however. They hadn't fucked. Not even when she had quivered under him in surrender, her tight heat milking his fingers, her soft little sounds driving him wild and inviting him to take her.

He had stopped even though it killed him. Even though he had wanted to drive deep inside her until he couldn't remember his own name. Until he forgot the guilt eating at him.

This was salvageable. He could forget what they had done, the way she felt. The way she tasted … like honey and butter on his tongue.

"What am I supposed to think, Cullen?" she demanded. "This was a difficult night for you. I was a welcome distraction. And combined with alcohol …" She shook her head, her mane of dark blonde hair tossing around her shoulders. "It explains a lot about what happened between us."

He resisted insisting what happened between them had been coming from day one. Ever since Beck demanded he come and meet his sister and help her move in. He was screwed the minute she stepped outside her house. Dressed in blue jeans and a Georgia State University sweatshirt, she was your squeaky-clean girl next door. Her long blonde ponytail bounced as she jogged down the steps to greet them. He had hesitated behind Beck, taking in her makeup-free face.

When she turned those blue eyes on him he felt like someone punched him in the gut. She was sweet and innocent. A regular Girl Scout and yet all he could think about was getting her on all fours and taking her hard and fast and dirty. He was one sick bastard. His first glance at his friend's sister and he wanted to ruin her, and tonight he had finally come close to doing that.

It dawned on him that she was giving him a way out. An

excuse to pardon tonight's actions. They could get beyond the fact that he had felt her up like she was some girl in the backseat of his high school Bronco and pretend this never happened.

A horn honked outside.

She bolted for the door. "I'll see you at the ceremony tomorrow."

He lunged after her, stalling her at the door with a hand on her arm. "I'll walk you out."

She opened her mouth like she wanted to protest, but he didn't stick around to hear it. He opened the door and strode outside, heedless that he was barefoot. He released a sigh of relief at the sight of the driver. A harried-looking woman, not a day younger than sixty, sat behind the wheel. She jerked her chin at him in greeting.

He opened the door for Huntley, feeling safer knowing she was in the cab with the older female rather than some strange man.

She paused before ducking in. "See you tomorrow?"

He nodded. "Sure. Tomorrow. Thanks for babysitting me."

She averted her gaze, nodding. "No problem. That's what I'm here for."

*That's what I'm here for.* To babysit him? He swallowed a growl. She probably wasn't talking about letting him feel her up.

His gaze crawled over her face and hot color suffused her cheeks. He knew she was remembering it all in that moment. His mouth on her, his fingers. His dick stirred. Hell. How were things ever supposed to go back to normal between them now when all he wanted to do was follow through on where his mouth and fingers had been?

Because there was no other choice. They were friends and he needed to make sure they stayed that way.

"See you tomorrow." He nodded.

She slammed the door shut behind her and the car pulled away from the curb. He watched the taillights fade down the street and turn the corner.

He stared, peering unseeingly into the night for several moments before returning inside to his empty house. Empty bed.

Pulling the sheets up to his waist, he closed his eyes and tried to pretend like he couldn't still smell her all around him. When he took himself in hand and started stroking, he told himself it was a simple release he was after and it had nothing to do with her specifically. He clung to that lie until the moment he climaxed and it was only her face in his mind.

# CHAPTER FIVE

Huntley picked up Beck and took him to an early dinner. It was good to have a little time alone together. Even if it was hard to meet his gaze after last night, knowing what she had done with his best friend, knowing what she had allowed his best friend to do to her. Allowed? Hell, she had reveled in it.

"Mom wants you to come home," he announced over his burger. "And everyone else does too."

She nodded, finishing her juice in a long sip. "I know."

And by everyone he meant *everyone*. They had aunts, uncles and cousins by the truckloads. Everyone also meant Jackson. Her ex kept up with her online and via text. He liked to call her between his breakups and remind her that once upon a time they had planned to spend their futures together and that even though he dumped her she was still in the running for his future wife. His coaxing voice had the opposite effect on her, however. A future with him meant she had to fit into his idea of what she should be. Jackson loved her as long as she placed him at the center of the universe. He never wanted her to work. He expected her to put him before everything and everyone.

"I know."

"So why don't you then?"

"I like my job." That was one reason.

"And that's enough to stay here? Even if our entire family is halfway across the country? Are you dating anyone? Last time we talked—"

"No. I'm not seeing anyone." An image of Cullen's face hovering above her in the near dark of his room flashed through her mind and sent a warm blast of heat her.

"Then think about it, Huntley. You shouldn't be here all alone without any family around you."

It was on the tip of her tongue to remind him that she had Cullen. She wasn't alone. Beck himself had appointed him as her watchdog, after all, but then she stopped herself. She didn't *have* Cullen. No one had Cullen. And after last night, he'd probably treat her with the cool distance he treated every one-night stand. He'd be Sullen Cullen, even to her.

"Hey, you okay, Hunt?"

She forced a bright smile. "Sure. Now, let's go get you that medal." She reached across the table and dusted a speck of lint off his dress uniform shoulder. "I'm proud of you, you know."

He grinned. "And I'm proud of you, little sister.

She rolled her eyes. "Seventeen minutes."

"I'm still older."

"Keep lording that over me." Smiling, she looked out the diner window. "This place feels like home now."

She didn't want to go back just to get sucked into that world again. She liked what she had here. She winced, realizing a lot of her life here was wrapped up in Cullen, and if she wanted things to return to normal, she needed to clear the air between them and put last night behind them for good.

"I'll try to explain it to the family," Beck said as he tossed down money on the table and slid out from the booth. "But I can't promise they're not going to continue to nag you about it."

Nodding, she led the way to where she parked her car. "You sure you want to go back? Even with Mary there?"

He nodded. "I'm not scared of facing her. I've moved on." Beck sounded truly unaffected. He really wasn't broken up over Mary cheating on him and dumping him. He settled into the passenger seat and stared ahead out the window, tapping his thigh with an almost anxious energy.

"You okay?" she asked.

"Fine. Why?"

Huntley shook her head. "You just seem different."

He smiled slightly and rubbed at his chin. There was something elusive in the curve of his mouth. There was a time in her life when she could practically read his thoughts—and he hers. Right now she couldn't get a read on him. He was keeping something from her.

Suddenly the thought of what *she* was keeping from *him* hit her full force and she was grateful they couldn't read each other quite as well as they used to. Heat flamed her face as the memory of Cullen's fingers touching her, filling her, swept over her. Fast on the heels of that memory followed longing for something longer and harder of his to fill her.

Her fingers clenched tighter around the steering wheel. She stared straight ahead, inhaling and fighting back the fire in her face as she pulled into the parking lot and found a spot. Turning off the engine, they both stepped out in the afternoon and started walking toward the building.

"Oh, hey, there's Cullen."

There were several other soldiers attired in dress uniform throughout the parking lot, but she identified Cullen instantly. Her gaze zoomed in on him as though he were a homing device.

Her pulse jack-knifed against her throat as her brother shouted out for his friend.

Cullen stopped and turned, his lean body strong and tall. He cut a fine figure in his uniform and all her girl parts tingled with awareness as they crossed the lot toward him. Sunshine glinted off the shiny buttons and medals on his uniform.

They stopped and she held silent as Beck and Cullen shook hands. She scarcely breathed as they exchanged greetings.

Cullen's dark eyes were cool and distant as they settled on her. "Hey, Huntley."

She forced a smile. "Cullen."

She fell in beside her brother as they entered the building. Cullen and Beck stopped every few feet, greeting people they knew. She stood by patiently, trying not to devour the sight of Cullen. He was so hot it hurt to look at him. Not that it stopped other women from looking. Every female in the vicinity did double takes of Cullen and her brother, lust and admiration bright in their gazes. She wanted to slap them. Or worse. She wanted to walk up beside Cullen and put her hand on him in some way that marked him as hers. Yeah, that was definitely worse. And ridiculous.

Beck led her to a seat at the front of the auditorium.

After a quick kiss on her cheek, Beck left and took his place up on the stage. Cullen left her, too, moving off to talk to another man in his dress uniform. Voices buzzed around her as others found their seats. She crossed her legs and settled her hands on her lap, staring straight ahead and wishing this thing would get started so she didn't have to focus on the fact that Cullen seemed to be giving her the cold shoulder. Or maybe he was just doing what he did after he fooled around with a woman. A painful thought. He had never treated her to Sullen Cullen before, and she didn't like it. Not one bit.

* * *

She smelled good. She looked good.

These two thoughts bounced around inside his head as the ceremony began. He couldn't bring himself to sit beside her, so he deliberately waited until it was too late, until all the seats were occupied and he was forced to remain standing along the edges of the auditorium.

He supposed he should count it as a blessing that he was so wrapped up in her and how pretty she looked in her dress that he could barely concentrate on what else was happening. Even when the ceremony began, he found himself staring at her sitting there in her coral-colored dress with the heart-shaped bodice that showed just a hint of cleavage, but it was enough. Enough to make him want to haul her somewhere private where he could tug down the little cap sleeves and bare her for his hungry mouth.

Suddenly he noticed Beck was talking behind the podium, accepting the Silver Star. He listened to Beck's words, listened as he dedicated the medal to Xander, and felt something loosen inside his chest. A small measure of peace maybe.

He also noticed the woman sidling up beside him. He glanced at her and then away before his gaze jerked back. It was Mary, Beck's ex-girlfriend. He'd met her a few times before Beck deployed. Beck looked equally surprised to see her, pausing as he descended from the stage. Cullen's gaze sought out Huntley. She looked shocked, as well, and decidedly *not* thrilled to see the girl who stomped all over her brother's heart. In fact, she looked like a mama bear ready to tear Mary apart as she intercepted Beck. She rose from her chair and stormed in their direction.

Cullen grabbed her arm, stopping her as Beck and Mary slipped out through one of the auditorium's exit doors.

She tugged on her arm. "The nerve of her coming all the way here after what she did—"

"Give them some privacy."

She glared at him. "Let me go—"

"Are you going to go after them?"

Her mouth pursed mulishly.

He shook his head down at her. "Your brother is a grown man and can fight his own battles."

"I know that, but Mary just isn't some girl he dated. They've been together forever. She was my friend first. Did you know that? Since kindergarten. She betrayed us all when she betrayed him."

Cullen held her stormy blue gaze for a moment before nodding and letting go of her arm.

She looked toward the door where they departed and then back at him. "Fine." Crossing her arms over her chest, she leaned against the wall beside him. "I'll give them a couple of minutes and then nothing is stopping me from following and giving her a piece of my mind."

A smile twitched his lips.

"What's so funny?" she snapped.

"I've never seen you like this."

"Like what?"

"Mad." Before he could consider it, he added, "It's kind of hot."

Color flooded her face, and suddenly all the tense awkwardness of last night was between them again. They were in his bed and his hands were on her skin, sliding her thighs apart, sinking into her satin heat, wringing soft little cries from her lips. He inhaled and smelled that fruit shampoo of hers. His gaze slipped down and he got caught up in the way the coral dress made her skin look lush as peaches. Lust slicked through him and he dropped his hands to disguise his sudden hard-on.

She stared straight ahead, nervously tucking a strand of hair behind her ear. "That's enough time." Turning, she made a beeline for the exit, the hem of her dress flirting around her knees.

# CHAPTER SIX

Huntley rounded the hallway and stopped hard. She didn't see Mary anymore. No. There was only her brother lip-locked with a dark-haired girl in a white lace dress. Well, that would explain the absence of Mary. He wasn't kidding when he said he was over his ex.

Not that it was hard to imagine him getting over Mary when he had this girl to help him along. She was vaguely familiar and Huntley thought she might have seen her around town. Maybe on base. She was beautiful. Edgy, even in white lace. Beck looked like he was going to pull her deep inside himself and never let go. Her hands crawled over Beck's massive shoulders, and it was clear she was all for that plan.

This girl was the reason for that elusive expression on her brother's face on the drive over. He was in love with her. She knew this about him just like she knew he loved banana and peanut butter sandwiches and spent the first eight years of his life with a Rambo poster on his wall.

Cullen came up beside her. She was assailed by his scent.

That faint hint of soap and laundry sheets and man. And something else. That *thing* she had smelled in his bed with him. A pheromone that belonged to him alone. Whatever it was, it shot a bolt of lust straight through her.

*God.* It was like she was a victim of her body. For a brief moment she was on her back again, his hand between her thighs, the salty musk of his skin swirling all around her. She salivated as though she was hungry. Starving. Only not for food. For him. For what he could give her. Last night had been a sample. *Sometimes it gets a little rough.* She knew there was more. So much more to be had. His body was built for pleasure, and she knew he would have sex like he did everything else. With focus and intensity and power.

"I don't think he's going to need a ride home," he murmured beside her.

"No," she said evenly, glad her voice came out normally. "Looks like he's got that covered."

Whatever was going on with her brother and this girl, it wasn't meaningless for him. Her chest hollowed out a little watching Beck make out with a girl whose name she didn't even know.

With Cullen beside her, she shifted nervously. She tried not to think about them. About them yesterday.

He had lit a fire within her. Stirred coals to life that had been long dormant. She needed to get laid and soon, before she threw herself at Cullen's feet and begged him to finish what he had started.

Cullen propped a hand on the wall, his arm brushing along her back. "Well, good for Beck."

She nodded, a lump forming in her throat. Yes. Good for her brother. He had found someone. He had been here all of three days and found someone. Meanwhile, she was a leper. Even Cullen didn't want to seal the deal. Last night she had been his for the taking and he had stopped.

"Yeah," she replied, hoping she didn't sound as shell-shocked as she felt.

"He deserves it."

She turned to face Cullen, suddenly not wanting to talk about her brother and the happiness he'd found. Yes, he deserved it. Yes, she wanted him to be happy. But right now it only reminded her of how she got a fat fail when it came to relationships.

Cullen's sculpted lips twitched like he wanted to smile, clearly pleased for her brother.

"And you don't, Cullen?" she asked.

He turned to face her, his mouth all hard and flat again, a faint question in his eyes.

"Deserve happiness," she clarified.

Okay, calling attention to his perpetual single status might not have been the way to go if she was trying to get things back on normal footing between them. She never questioned his lifestyle. She certainly didn't pressure him to get serious and date any of his one-night stands.

His eyes grew more hooded, the dark depths shielding whatever was going on inside his head. "Don't put me on your shrink's couch, Huntley. I'm satisfied with my life. I think it's you who isn't happy."

Cullen was right on that score. She'd joined a dating service because she wasn't happy with the status quo. He knew that. But at least she was working on changing her life. Grandma always said there was nothing wrong with taking a hard look at your life and not liking what you saw. The wrong was in doing nothing to fix it.

She glanced back at her brother, still lip-locked with his girl, his big hands cupping her face like she was the most treasured, special thing in the world to him. She wanted that for herself. Returning her gaze to Cullen, she knew she wasn't going to find that with him. Her stomach churned sickly. Suddenly that mattered a lot. It hurt. Even though she told herself not to let it, last night with him mattered.

Without another word, she turned and started down the long hallway. She'd text Beck later. She didn't want to interrupt what was obviously an intimate moment. Besides, she had a coffee date tonight that she needed to get ready for. The first step to fixing her life. Grandma would be proud.

Cullen's dress shoes clicked next to her. "Where are you headed?"

She tucked a strand of hair behind her ear, lifting one shoulder as she stepped out into fading sunlight, unwilling to tell him about her date for some reason. It felt weird confiding that after last night.

"Home. I'm kind of tired." She winced over the implication that she hadn't slept last night, but the words were out of her mouth before she could snatch them back.

He scanned the parking lot, his eyes squinting slightly against the sea of gleaming hoods and glinting windshields. "Guess I'm to blame for that."

"No blame," she quickly replied, her voice breathless. "It was a rough night. I get it." The word *rough* conjured other ideas too. Conversation. Memories. The surety of his movements. He didn't coax. He didn't ask for permission. His fingers claimed their place between her legs like they belonged there, as though it was his right. Her body had only responded with invitation, panting and moaning and clinging to the sheets like a woman begging to be ridden.

He'd made her feel so small and feminine. His big shoulders wedging between her legs along with his hand, his fingers. The ridge of his erection had felt bigger than anything she ever encountered.

A moan welled up from her chest, and she bit her lip to trap it inside.

He shook his head and snorted lightly. "It was still wrong of me."

Heat slapped her cheeks. That's what he was calling what happened between them. *Wrong.* She stopped beside her car, punching the unlock button. "It's okay. You were dealing with a heavy load yesterday and—"

"Don't treat me like I'm some fragile soul, Huntley." The warning rang in his voice. "Save that for your patients. I shouldn't have—"

"Oh, I know you're not fragile. Not an ounce of weakness in you." She clucked her tongue and leaned back against the side of her car, looking up at him. "Nuh-uh. You're the eternal soldier. Never weak. You carry the world on your shoulders and take the blame for everything."

Suddenly, she felt very tired. Who was she to think she had all the answers and could fix him? It was enough effort to carve the life she wanted for herself. She couldn't save him too.

She waved her hand slightly in a gesture of apology. "Look, let's just forget last night. We're friends." She laughed once. "You're probably the best friend I have here. I don't want to mess that up, and I don't want things to get weird."

A muscle feathered along his jaw. "Agreed then.

Let's just forget it."

She blinked and stared at him for a long moment. Squaring her shoulders, she tried not to feel offended that he could so easily forget it and move on when that was precisely what she was asking him to do.

"Good." She nodded stiffly. "I mean, we didn't even kiss." Okay, this would be the point where she stopped talking. "We did that other … stuff … but we've never even kissed." Sweet Jesus, she was babbling.

His head tilted to the side a fraction, his hooded eyes studying her, the corners of his well-carved mouth dipping as if that had not occurred to him. "No," he said softly, his voice a deep purr that stroked her skin. "We skipped that."

"Yeah." She continued nodding like one of those bobblehead dolls. "Right? We haven't even kissed, and that's the most basic form of making out, right? Like first base. We skipped first base, so. So …"

*God, Huntley, shut up.* Before she could insert her foot any deeper in her mouth, she whirled around and unlocked her door.

She pulled it open and her spine collided with his chest. "Oh, excuse me."

His warm breath gusted her cheek. She turned. His mouth was so close. Tantalizingly close. She caught a whiff of his mint toothpaste. Her gaze darted from his lips to his eyes, so dark and mesmerizing. They pulled her in, muddied her thoughts. She leaned in slightly, forgetting everything, wanting that mouth.

"Such a shame," he murmured. His thumb brushed her bottom lip and a bolt of lust shot through her body. "I should have tasted this mouth when I had the chance."

Desire licked through her, mingling with regret. He exerted more pressure on her bottom lip, parting her mouth so that his thumb dipped between her lips. Her breathing hitched. She tasted him with her tongue, the barest, swirling stroke, and his eyes went black with heat. He closed the fraction of space between them, his chest grazing the front of her dress. Her breasts grew heavy and tight, aching. *Sweet Jesus, he was going to do it. Yes, yes, please.*

He dropped his hand and pulled back.

She fell back a step against her car, gulping a shuddering breath, fighting for composure. Tossing him a faltering smile, she slid inside her car. "Glad we had this talk."

He stared down at her, the heat in his eyes banked.

She offered him a tremulous smile. Everything was supposed to be fine between them now. There wasn't supposed to be any more weirdness or tension. Except for the fact that she couldn't quite catch her breath and her skin felt like it might catch fire.

She swallowed against the lump in her throat, desire still pumping through her and settling heavily between her legs. "I'll see you around." Ugh. Couldn't she project more confidence? It sounded more like a question than a statement.

He nodded, looking at her with his cold, hooded gaze. The dark, slashing brows over those deeply set eyes made her stomach dip and twist.

"Sure," he said, but his hand lingered on the frame like he was going to stop her, and a part of her wanted him to.

She wanted him to argue with her. To insist things could never go back to normal. To yank her door open and haul her out of the car, snatch her up in his arms and kiss her senseless.

Only he didn't do that. Of course not. She wasn't the irresistible sort that drove controlled men like Cullen to lose control. Last night had been an anomaly.

She tugged on her door and he let it go. It shut with a thud, sealing her in like she was protected within a little bubble. She on the inside. He outside.

With shaking hands, she turned her ignition and started the car. Still watching him, she backed out of her spot, her breath a ragged rattle in her chest. *Get it together, Huntley. You have a date.*

Training her gaze ahead, she drove away.

* * *

It took everything in Cullen not to march across the parking lot and get into his truck and follow her.

*Why the hell hadn't he kissed her?*

Now he was consumed with this regret, feverish for the taste of her he had missed.

*Shit.* He dragged a hand over his scalp. When it came to Huntley, he had ceased to think. The only thing guiding him was his cock. It was a real problem.

He could only replay her words in his head. *We didn't even kiss. We skipped first base.*

It was a fact he had been achingly aware of from the moment she left his house last night. He couldn't explain the oversight. Only that when he felt her back her ass into him, he could only think of getting his hands on her, sliding his fingers inside her heat, touching her where he imagined burying his dick.

Her words served to taunt and challenge him simultaneously. He knew she didn't intend for that, but her intention didn't matter. There was only what he felt. The need to chase her, pin her down and take. Claim. Finish what they began. This possessiveness was a wholly new experience for him. It never happened with other women, and he knew it was because Huntley wasn't like other women for him.

Cursing, he retreated to his truck and headed home. Once there, he changed and took a run, pounding out his frustration on asphalt in the fading light of day until sweat clung to him.

He pushed himself until his muscles burned, and then he turned back and ran the remaining miles home. He sought exhaustion. Bone-deep weariness. Maybe if he were good and tired, he wouldn't spend the rest of the night thinking about her.

That plan lasted until he returned to his empty house and took a shower. Walking into his bedroom, he glanced at the clock. Five minutes past seven.

Immediately, he had a vision of Huntley sitting at Java Joe's, nursing her steaming mug with whatever latest book she was reading in one of the coffeehouse's comfy, well-worn armchairs. She was probably there now. He usually joined her. He chalked it up to doing his part, keeping his promise to Beck and keeping an eye out for her.

But Beck was back now. *You don't have to go there and babysit her.*

He pulled a black T-shirt on with angry movements, wondering why that didn't seem to matter to him. He grabbed his keys and headed out the door. He knew he should probably give them both some space after yesterday.

God knew he needed perspective. Or maybe a quick hookup with someone else to help him shake off this unacceptable bout of lust he was feeling toward her.

And yet the image of Huntley sitting alone in Java Joe's spurred him on.

He told himself he was going there for her, because he couldn't stand the thought of her sitting all by herself. Because he was her closest friend in this town.

Not because he wanted to see her again. Not because he craved more of last night.

Not because he intended to have her.

# CHAPTER SEVEN

"You're a lot prettier than your picture."

Huntley forced a smile at the compliment. "Thank you." *And you look shorter in person.* The thought skidded through her mind as she swapped pleasantries with her date. They stood at the coffee bar, waiting for their drinks. She chafed one hand up and down her arm, pretending not to notice him checking her out.

"I bet your patients never want to go home," he continued. "Security probably has to drag them out of the ER."

She smiled again, wondering if they were going to move beyond the inane compliments. According to his profile, they had a lot in common. When were they going to start clicking?

Her favorite barista, Sheridan, set her drink down before her, her purple-tipped red hair bobbing stylishly above her shoulders as she moved. "Here you go, Huntley."

"Thanks, Sheridan." She picked up her mug and met

the girl's inquisitive gaze. In the years Huntley had been frequenting Java Joe's she had never brought a man here. Well, other than Cullen, of course.

"And here's yours." Sheridan slid a mug at Greg, her smile slipping. For whatever reason, she did not bestow her usual perky smile on him.

Greg accepted his drink. When his phone started pinging, he fumbled for it in his blazer pocket. Glancing at the screen, he looked up at Huntley through his wire-rimmed glasses. He was cute in a scholarly way. Not muscular. Not a soldier. Her hands might even be larger than his. His hands definitely weren't like Cullen's big, capable mitts. Nor like his long, deft fingers that stroked—

STOP. She gave her head a single swift shake. This was the kind of guy she was looking for. Someone gentle and academic, cerebral, who liked to spend his free time at libraries. According to his profile, he made an epic goat cheese frittata.

It would be nice, after a day of mayhem, to return to a home-cooked meal. An image of Cullen's big body over hers, his hand working between her thighs, making her shudder out her release, flashed across her mind. *Sweet Jesus, yes. That would be nice at the end of a hard day too.*

"Would you pardon me? It's my on-call service."

She blinked, chasing away the inappropriate thoughts. "Of course."

He ducked toward the back of the coffeehouse.

"Who's the tool?" Sheridan leaned over the bar to inquire.

Huntley huffed. "He's a dentist. And very nice."

"That so? Where's Cullen?"

Her face flushed. "It's not my day to watch him."

Sheridan held up both hands as though to ward off an attack. "Sorry, sorry. Don't be so touchy. Just thought that there was something between you two—"

"We're just friends. You know that."

Sheridan snorted. "Friends with benefits, you mean?"

"No!" She sent a quick look to where her date talked in the corner. He lifted his chin and waved back at her. "It's not like that with us," she insisted. *Last night it almost turned into that though.*

"Well, it should be like that. I've watched you two flirting around it forever. I don't know what's stopping you from crawling all over that man and licking him from top to bottom."

Huntley rolled her eyes. "It's not that simple. We're just friends," she insisted, nervously tracing the rim of her cup.

"Does Cullen know that?"

She nodded. "Of course. And he knows I'm dating." In a way.

"Really? As in, he knows you're on a date right now? Because here he comes. We should ask him."

Huntley's head swiveled to watch as Cullen stepped inside the coffeehouse. Gone was his dress uniform. He was wearing a pair of well-worn, faded jeans and a snug black T-shirt that did amazing things to his chest. Okay, maybe that chest did amazing things for his shirt.

His gaze landed on her. Sheridan leaned closer across the bar to whisper, "Mmm-mm, that man," she nodded once, "is hotter than two mice fucking in a wool sock, and if I were you I would hop on him."

Huntley didn't even blink at the girl's colorful speech. She fixed her gaze on Cullen as he advanced.

He stopped before her. "Hey."

"Hey, Cullen," Sheridan chimed. "Your usual?"

He gave her a quick glance before looking back at Huntley. "Yes, thanks."

"What are you doing here?" Huntley blurted, resisting looking over her shoulder to Greg.

He shrugged. "It's Wednesday. What's so unusual about me being here?"

Not that unusual, but she hadn't expected it. She'd already seen so much of him lately, and with Beck here he didn't need to hold himself up to the same standard of watchdog-ness. She thought she would have been safe.

She had the insane urge to throw a coat over Greg as though that would somehow hide him. Ridiculous, of course. She had no reason to hide the fact that she was on a date. In fact, *let* Cullen see she was dating. Then he'd know she wasn't clinging to last night . . . that everything was truly fine and normal and there wasn't any lingering weirdness between them.

The decision was taken out of her hands when Greg returned, stuffing his phone back in his blazer pocket. "Ah, sorry about that." He stopped at her side, his hand coming to rest at her elbow.

She pasted a wobbly smile on her lips. "That's okay."

Cullen tensed, his gaze moving from her to Greg, his cold eyes pointedly dropping to the hand that clasped her elbow.

"Here you go, Cullen," Sheridan's voice intruded as she offered Cullen his usual coffee.

Cullen dug into his pocket and removed his wallet. Without removing his gaze from Huntley and Greg, he offered a few dollars to Sheridan. "Keep the change."

"Cullen, this is Greg." Huntley motioned to Greg. There was no getting around introductions now. "Cullen is my … friend."

She could kick herself for the pause there. She almost had said her brother's friend, but the way she had paused he probably thought she was looking for some other filler word. *This is Cullen, the guy I made out with last night who gets all my girl parts torqued up.*

Cullen stared hard at her for a moment before shaking hands with Greg.

Greg did a quick assessment of Cullen, not missing the cropped dark hair or glint of dog tags. If she wasn't mistaken, Greg's nostrils flared as though he had encountered something tainted.

She shifted on her feet, feeling a surge of defensiveness. As though she needed to protect Cullen, which was crazy. He was the least vulnerable person she knew. Even hurting over losing Xander, his veneer was rock solid. Greg's opinion of him wouldn't affect him in the least.

"How about the table by the window, Huntley?" Greg suggested, urging her along, his gaze on her, Cullen forgotten.

"Sure." She nodded, reminding herself this was a date.

"See you later, Cullen." Together she and Greg weaved between tables and took their seats.

She tried to focus on Greg as he dove into a story about himself. The back of her neck prickled. She reached a hand there and rubbed self-consciously, trying to concentrate on Greg. A good half hour passed and the situation was unbearable. She told herself it was because of Cullen. If he wasn't here, she could enjoy herself on her first date in forever.

She felt Cullen behind her. Felt his stare. She heard the higher feminine tone of Sheridan's voice and the deep rumble from Cullen as he replied, and her stomach pitched. Huntley crossed her legs and then uncrossed them again beneath the table, resisting the urge to look over her shoulder.

"So I know this town is full of Army meatheads," Greg was saying, "but the cost of living here is great, and there aren't too many dentists to compete with." He stopped for a breath and it looked like he might let her get a word in. "What about you? How did you end up here?"

"Well, my twin brother is a meathead actually. He completed his training here and helped get me a job at the hospital on base before he was deployed."

"Oh." An awkward silence fell between them. She rubbed at the back of her neck again, still feeling Cullen's eyes drilling into her.

She forced herself to swallow the last bit of her latte. She tapped the rim of her mug idly. "Well, this has been nice." Her voice squeaked a little at the end of the lie in an attempt to sound perky. As though this really had been nice and not all shades of uncomfortable. She reached for her handbag looped around the back of her chair.

"Yeah." Greg pushed to his feet the same time she did. "I had a really good time, too. Maybe next time we can do dinner? There's a great French bistro that just opened."

"Sure." She lifted one shoulder even though staying home alone and curling up on the couch sounded more tempting. "Just email me." She supposed she should try at least one more date with him before calling it quits. She wasn't going to meet anyone if she was too picky.

"Great." Beaming, he settled his hand on the small of

her back and led her from the coffeehouse.

As she stepped from the building and out into the warm sunshine, she risked one final glance behind her to the bar where Cullen sat perched on a stool.

He was still there as she knew he would be, one palm pressed flat on top of the counter beside his cup, his other arm hanging loosely at his side. It was a casual pose. Almost listless. And yet it wasn't. Tightly leashed energy radiated off him as he sat there. He reminded her of an animal, frozen for an endless moment before he sprang into action. The sight made her pulse thrum faster at her neck.

She squared her shoulders. He had no reason to be angry, and she had no reason to feel like she had done something wrong. They were friends, moving on from one little misstep.

Greg stepped closer. His face was near enough that she could make out the slight overlap of his front tooth over its neighbor and she couldn't help thinking it ironic that a dentist would have less-than-perfect teeth.

"W-what are you doing?" she stammered.

"Would it be okay if I kissed you?"

A swift "no" rose to her lips. She hardly knew him. Forgetting that fact, she didn't *want* to kiss him. He might not be ugly, but he was the last man she wanted to kiss. The man she wanted to kiss sat inside that coffeehouse, watching her.

*Watching her.*

If Cullen saw another man kiss her, then he couldn't possibly think she was hung up on him. She seized upon this idea. Somehow it made perfect sense to her.

"Yes," she blurted before she fully considered the consequences.

Greg's eyes lit up like he was presented with an unexpected toy. He worked his mouth as though getting ready for some heavy-duty lip action and closed the distance separating them. He flattened his mouth on hers.

It wasn't a terrible kiss. No tongue action, thankfully, but he clung to her bottom lip for a long moment like he wanted to take it with him. Maybe he thought it was sexy, but it just felt ... odd.

When they stepped apart, he smiled. "See you soon."

She nodded, forcing herself not to look through the glass door for Cullen. She couldn't. It would reveal that she perhaps had an ulterior motive in kissing Greg. Which she did, but she didn't want Cullen to know that.

With a final goodbye for Greg, she hurried to her car. She felt a grim sense of satisfaction knowing she had given Cullen evidence that she wasn't sitting at home pining for him—or working her vibrator raw lusting after him. She was a big girl, taking her own life by the horns. Still. Her chest ached in a way that felt far from okay.

She slid behind the wheel, started her engine and backed out of her spot without even yet buckling. Almost as though she expected him to give chase. Of course he wouldn't. There would be no reason for that.

She glanced at herself in the rearview mirror, noting her flushed face and overly bright eyes. It had nothing to do with Greg and everything to do with Cullen.

Lowering her gaze, she wiped a hand over the back of her mouth, ridding herself the memory of Greg's mouth there. It had been necessary, but she still longed for Cullen. His lips, his taste to erase and replace all others.

As she departed the parking lot, the pulse at her neck

steadied, and a hollow feeling spread throughout her chest as she realized that she might not be able to forget her night with Cullen. Ever.

At the first red light she reached, she managed to buckle her seatbelt. Staring blindly ahead, she wondered where this put her. If she couldn't stop wanting Cullen, craving him as more than a friend, where did that leave her?

How could they be friends at all?

# CHAPTER EIGHT

Cullen managed to cool his heels at Java Joe's for an entire five minutes after Huntley left. His hand opened and flexed at his side, the urge to hit something strong and crushing inside him. Huntley on a date was bad enough. Watching her kiss that asshat … that was worse.

"So. You're totally just going to sit here like that whole thing didn't bother you?"

He shot a glance at Sheridan as she prepared someone's drink. "Why would I be bothered?"

She snorted. "Right. You spent the last few years hanging out with Huntley and now she shows up with a date. Not a big deal."

"We're just friends."

"Is that what you call it these days?"

Shaking his head, he stood up from the barstool. "See you later."

"Keep it real," she called as he headed outside and made his way to his truck. He started for home, but his mind rebelled, wondering if Huntley was going to see that tool again.

He beat the steering wheel once with a curse. He couldn't believe she had let that guy kiss her. Sure, she was single and free to give her lips to any man she wanted, but after last night was she really so eager to be with someone else? She was the only female he could think about. The only one he wanted.

*Maybe you got her primed and she's looking to seal the deal with someone else.*

"Fuck," he growled and turned his truck around in a hard U-turn that broke a dozen traffic violations. He didn't care. He pushed his foot on the accelerator without even thinking, only one destination in mind.

* * *

She had just changed into one of her favorite softest T-shirts and yoga pants, scrubbed off her makeup, pulled her hair up into a ponytail and began the stare-down with her refrigerator, contemplating a snack of cheese cubes and yogurt, when the knock rapped at her front door.

A quick look through the peephole revealed Cullen standing there, one hand braced somewhere to the right of the door. She gasped. *Sweet Jesus.* He even looked hot through the peephole. She jerked away from the door, her hand flying to her mouth. She suddenly regretted taking off her makeup. Rolling her eyes, she mentally called herself ten shades of fool. Cullen had seen her without makeup before.

"Open the door, Huntley." His deep, steady voice sent a bolt of heat down her spine. For a split second, she contemplated refusing and then shame flushed through her. This was Cullen. No matter what had transpired between them, whatever path she chose in life, she could trust him. He was a good guy. Even if he didn't know it, he always did the right thing. And in this case, as far as he was concerned, the right thing was keeping his hands off her.

With a deep breath, she pulled open the door. "Cullen." Was that breathy squeak actually her voice? She swallowed and tried again. "What are you doing here?"

A muscle ticked in his jaw, and she realized that was a rather inane question. She never asked him why he stopped by. She simply opened her door, her home, her heart to him, no questions asked. Every time. It was just further proof how different things were between them. How they might never be the same again.

He didn't answer, didn't move from outside her doorway. His liquid-dark gaze skimmed her up and down, not missing the well-worn T-shirt, yoga pants and bare toes burrowing into the carpet.

"I forgot something," he muttered.

"Oh?"

He nodded once. "Yeah."

It was like someone pushed a pause button. Time yawned, ticking in silence. Neither moved. Tension thickened the air between them. She couldn't even breathe as his gaze speared her.

Then a switch flipped.

His hand looped around her neck and he hauled her against him, simultaneously stepping inside her house. His mouth crashed over hers. *Cullen was kissing her.* It was everything and nothing like she ever fantasized.

Hard and soft. Sweet and lethal. His firm, warm lips slanted against hers. His tongue slid inside and she gasped.

She felt consumed. Branded.

Dimly, she registered the click of the door, but she could hardly keep up with things like the door shutting or Cullen backing her into the living room with his mouth moving on hers.

She couldn't breathe. Her chest felt like it was going to explode at the heady scent of him, the taste … at the stroke of his velvet tongue against hers. She was overcome, stunned senseless, her lips motionless.

He pulled back slightly and growled against her lips. "Kiss me, Huntley."

His words broke something loose inside her. Ignited her. She leaned into his mouth, kissing him back, ravenous, touching her tongue to his.

He made a deep growl of approval, bent and then lifted her off her feet. She squeaked and gripped his shoulders. "Cullen!" she cried against his lips, "I'm too—"

"I'm not dropping you," he rasped on her mouth. "Not ever."

Her heart tripped as she realized he was carrying her with ease toward her bedroom, his big hands holding her up by her bottom, his mouth still devouring hers.

He brought her down on her bed, coming over her, his hands flattening on either side of her head, caging her in. He lifted his head and the air left her in a rush as she looked up into his starkly handsome face.

His gaze drilled into her. "I've been thinking I needed to rectify what you said earlier and kiss you."

"Oh. You did that." She waited, half expecting him to

push off the bed and call it good between them. They had kissed, after all. And then some.

He stood and her heart sank to realize she was right, but he didn't move away. He stared down at her, his dark eyes full of an emotion she couldn't read.

She sat up, pushing the tendrils of hair off her face that had come loose from her ponytail. She moistened her lips, reaching for her composure—the last of which fled as she watched him reach behind his neck and pull his shirt over his head in one smooth motion.

Her mouth dried at this sight of him. His shoulders and biceps looked like they were cut from marble. The muscled pecs, the ridged stomach. She'd seen him without his shirt before, but never like this. Never like a hungry beast poised over her and ready to devour. He wasn't done with her. That much was clear. And she didn't want him to be.

She wanted to be devoured.

He seized the hem of her T-shirt and pulled it over her head. Cool air wafted over her. His eyes gleamed darkly as he eyed her in her simple white bra. Her stomach tightened when his fingers went to the front center clasp and flicked it open. Her breasts sprang free.

Heat scored her cheeks. She didn't remember ever being so on display for a man before. The number of men to see her breasts had been few and never in full light like this. Her hands came up to cover herself and he grabbed her wrists, tugging them back down. "No way are you going to hide from me."

The words acted like flint to steel, igniting a steady burn to all her most intimate parts. Her nipples tightened, pebbling into hard points, and her sex clenched, eager to be filled.

He came over her again, backing her down on the bed. Both his knees settled between her thighs, the mattress dipping with his weight. The denim of his jeans rasped against the soft cotton of her yoga pants. His stare slicked over her, feasting on her breasts before crawling down the slope of her stomach. He flattened one broad hand on her belly. His long fingers reached as far as her ribcage. He shifted and his fingertips grazed the undersides of her breasts.

She sucked in a sharp breath, arching her spine, singed at the touch. He wasn't like most guys. His greedy hands didn't dive for her breasts, squeezing and groping them like melons. He made her wait.

Both his hands spanned her torso as he leaned over her. His mouth a hairsbreadth from hers. She lifted her head off the bed, seeking his mouth, eager for him to kiss her again.

His words brushed over her. "You want my mouth again?"

She nodded and leaned closer.

He dodged her lips.

She made a sound of complaint and brought her hands to his shoulders. He plucked them off him and pinned them to the bed. Hard. He laced his fingers with hers and aligned their hips, his erection directly over her core. "I don't know… seems like anyone will do. You sure you want me to kiss you?"

He rocked against her, rubbing his hard length along the crotch of her yoga pants, knowing exactly what he was doing to her.

"I want you to kiss me," she insisted.

"You sure?"

She nodded.

He pressed her wrists into the bed and brought his mouth against her neck, directly beneath her ear. She felt his words vibrate against her skin. "Don't you *ever* kiss another man in front of me again."

She nodded even though a part of her rebelled at being told what to do. Cullen wielded total control over her and she reveled in it. For the first time she felt like she could let go. She was ready to submit entirely to a man, knowing that he would only deliver her pleasure.

His mouth dragged down her neck in a trail of biting kisses. Lips, grazing tongue and softly nipping teeth. She whimpered, wiggling under him, out of her mind with need. He reached where her neck and shoulder met, his warm breath fanning in the hollow there for an agonizing moment. Anticipation zipped through her as she waited for more. She trembled, holding her breath for his kiss there… for the slight scrape of teeth.

Finally it came. His teeth sank deep where her neck and shoulder met, marking her, claiming her. A choked gasp ripped from her as her bones liquefied and a rush of heat pooled between her legs. Her eyes flew wide and she gasped, positive no man had bitten her before. She had no idea she would like it so much. Had no idea she would feel it so deeply. He pulled back, laving the tender flesh with his tongue and feathering with his lips.

Her head was spinning, chest lifting with ragged breaths as his hand closed around one breast, lifting the generous swell toward his dipping head. The gentle pressure of his fingers on her flesh made her moan. She arched, desperate for him to take her in his mouth. She ran one hand over the back of his skull, tugging him down with an animal sound that she didn't even know herself capable of.

The tip of his tongue lightly stroked her nipple. "You want me to kiss you here? Think you deserve that?"

She writhed under him and almost came out of her skin as he dragged the rough pad of a thumb over the turgid peak. Her breast grew heavy in his hand. The one he neglected to even touch yet screamed for his attention, beyond swollen and achy.

His warm breath gusted over the aching tip. Anticipation zinged through her, warring with frustration. She needed this. Needed him. Annoyance sparked along her nerve.

"Maybe I should kiss other men," she flung out.

He tensed over her, his muscled shoulders turning to solid rock.

"It got you here, didn't it, Cullen?" she demanded. "Us here? Like this? Would you even be here if I hadn't kissed that guy in front of you?"

His hand slid down her belly to cup between her legs. She pulsed against his palm, her sex clenching for him to fill her. "You don't have to go to such lengths. If you wanted me in your bed, why didn't you say so sooner?"

His hot, dark gaze fixed on her face as he lowered and finally claimed her nipple, drawing it in the wet warmth of his mouth as his hand slid under the waistband of her yoga pants, delving smoothly beneath her underwear to stroke along her crease.

It was sensation overload. His teeth scored her nipple, and she screamed as he plunged one finger inside her. She came apart beneath him. Bright shards of colors exploded behind her eyelids.

"That's right, sweetheart. Come for me."

She nodded, unintelligible words tripping from her as he worked a second finger inside. "This is where I want to be, Huntley."

"Yes," she breathed.

His eyes locked with hers, dark and endless, peering inside her. He hopped up from the bed. She watched as he unsnapped his jeans and shoved them down over his hips, taking his briefs with them.

Her mouth dried. He stood over her, his cock jutting out, alarming in its size.

"Oh," she breathed.

She couldn't even circle him with one hand. She instinctively scooted back on the bed. "I'm not sure that is going to work."

"Oh, it's going to work, sweetheart." He reached for her and grabbed the waistband of her yoga pants, sliding them off her in one smooth motion, leaving her naked. The urge to shield herself came over her, and she closed her knees, angling her legs to the side. "You trust me?"

She did. Irrevocably. She trusted him. Cared about him. More than she should. For years now, she had harbored feelings for him. Desire, lust that she thought he could never reciprocate. But he did.

His warm hands closed over her knees, parting her legs and coming between them again. This time there was no rasp of denim against her. It was bare skin to bare skin, his callused palms an erotic scrape running along the insides of her thighs.

She was putty, ready and open for him. His fingers rubbed over her, and she was so wet her face burned with embarrassment.

His husky voice fanned her lips. "See. Your body wants this."

He gripped that enormous cock and rubbed it along her crease. She moaned and tilted her hips, ready for him to push inside her. He dragged his plump head up to her clit and rubbed in fierce circles.

She reached between them, dying to touch him. "Let me."

His hand drifted away and she closed her fingers around him, not surprised at his girth. She knew she would not be able to fully circle his erection in her hand.

A hissed breath escaped him. She exulted in grasping this strong, gorgeous man, controlling him as he had controlled her with his mouth and hands. She guided the tip of him to her opening, teasing him there, granting him the slightest entrance before stopping and pulling him back out.

"Enough teasing," he growled, his hand clamping on her wrist. "I can't wait."

"Then don't." She squeezed his cock and guided him in a little bit more, the head of him almost fully lodged inside her now, just in the threshold, already stretching her more than she had ever been stretched.

"Let me get a condom—"

"I'm on the pill," she said, her voice breathless. She had been on the pill ever since she was seventeen. Her doctor had prescribed it to help with cramps and the occasional breakouts. "Are you … okay?" She winced, hating the awkwardness of that question.

"I'm clean, but you don't have to do this." Sweat beaded the top of his lip, and she knew his control was slipping. "I've never been inside a woman before without a condom."

And that sealed it for her. She would be his first in this. Her heart swelled. She wanted to be the first woman to ever truly feel Cullen inside her. The first to have that with him, from him. "I trust you," she whispered.

Indecision warred on his face. She shifted her hips and tried to take more of him in. He held back, denying her.

"Don't you want inside me, Cullen?" She reached around him to grip his ass, digging her fingernails into the firm flesh, mindless in her hunger for him, urging him to drive deep. "With nothing between us."

He groaned and dropped his hand away from where he gripped himself. "Damn, Huntley … to know what it feels like to come inside you? To feel you milking my bare-skinned cock? *Yes*."

She didn't have time to draw air before he buried himself deep with one clean stroke.

She gasped and stiffened against the sudden invasion, her hands flying to his biceps. She was no virgin, but this definitely felt alien. She'd never felt anything like him. It was as though she was *full* of him, stuffed to the seams.

He dropped his head against her shoulder, his voice rumbling against her skin. "You feel so good, Huntley. Amazing."

She inhaled a bracing breath, adjusting to the sheer size of him pulsing in her.

He looked down at her. "Are you okay?"

"Yeah. Just been a while." She inhaled and exhaled several times. "And you're bigger than I'm used to."

He grinned, the smile slow and sexy. "You'll get used to it."

He bent his head, lifting one breast and drawing the

nipple deep, sucking and scoring it lightly with his teeth.

Her sex clenched, and she moaned at the sensation of his incredible hardness filling her, wedged so tight inside her channel that he felt like he was a part of her. As though there was no ending deciphering where he ended and she began. She arched her throat on a moan.

"Ah, I feel that. See? You *are* milking my cock."

She tossed her head in a wild nod and worked her hips under him, willing him to move. "Yes."

"You ready now?" He pinched her nipple between strong fingers, sending an arrow of lancing sensation right to where their bodies joined.

"Yes," she panted.

"What? What is it you're ready for?"

"Your cock … moving, fucking me."

"With pleasure," he growled, pulling out and pushing back in. Still controlled. Still steady. He kept it up, creating an even tempo of friction that had her writhing and moaning beneath him.

"What? What do you want, Huntley?"

"Harder."

His eyes darkened. "Hell yeah," he muttered, like it was all he was waiting for her to say.

His hands seized her hips and his pace increased. He pounded into her, the headboard rattling against the wall with his every thrust.

She shouted his name and clawed his back. His grip on her hips tightened, fingers hard and deep on her flesh.

He lifted her pelvis until her ass was up off the bed, his cock diving deep, hitting the spot that shattered her. She came, her body jerking violently. He continued to hammer into her, relentless as a machine.

"Oh, that's beautiful. Come for me again, sweetheart." His hands slid from her hips to grip her ass. He massaged the rounded swells as he drove in and out of her.

It wasn't possible. She never orgasmed like this. With Jackson it had been rare and never more than one a night. This didn't happen.

"I can't … I never…" Her voice cracked.

"Yes, you can. You *will*." His voice stroked over her like a physical caress.

She started to tremble as he pumped in and out, his big hands kneading her bottom in a way that got her hotter and made that invisible fist tighten and twist low in her belly. She was close again, and strange little animal sounds tore from her throat. She lifted and rolled her hips, her movements becoming clumsy in her desperation.

Another climax swelled up inside her, starting deep, curling her toes into the mattress. She lifted her hips and the tension in her core snapped. Delicious sensations shot out to every nerve ending before ribboning back to where he hit that sweet spot again and again. She gulped back a cry. Holy hell. She could hardly find the right spot when she was working to get herself off.

He knew where to find it. Knew every place to touch. Knew exactly what to do to make her body sing. One hand left her ass to find her clit, his fingers rubbing and pinching as he slid in and out of her.

That's all it took. She shattered, coming again, quivering under him as his pace increased to a frenzy, their bodies smacking loudly. "I told you. That's it, sweetheart." His breathing changed—his movements becoming less graceful, urgent as he drove to his own release.

He cursed, surging deep and holding himself still as he came inside her. "Oh, Christ," he panted.

He gave another short thrust, his hand splayed on her belly in a way that made her feel marked, her body owned and well used in a way that was wholly new and not unwelcome.

He removed his hand on her stomach and slid free, dropping on his side, breathing heavily. Euphoria clung to her, leaving her slightly cloudy-headed.

*So this was what she had been missing.*

The instant the thought entered her head, she wondered how she would ever go without it again. Without him. Euphoria or not, she wasn't blind to the weirdness factor. She'd just had mind-blowing sex with her good friend. Oh, and he happened to be her brother's best friend.

Would he get up and leave now? Would they resume their friendship like this never happened. She held very still beside him, not sure how to react. What did one say in a situation like this? Should she get up and put on her clothes—

His arm reached out and wrapped around her waist, hauling her close, tucking her to his side. She darted a look at his face. His eyes were closed, but she knew he wasn't sleeping. Yet. She waited several moments to see if he was going to say anything.

After ten minutes passed on her digital clock, she sucked up the nerve and broke the silence, asking, "Have you eaten yet?"

His mouth curved slightly. "No."

"I have leftover spaghetti."

"Sounds good."

Smiling, she slid out from his arm and rose. Bending,

she snapped up her discarded shirt.

"You don't have to do that."

Pulling her shirt over her head, she looked down over her shoulder at him, arching an eyebrow in question.

"I'll just be undressing you again later."

Heat flushed through her as his words rumbled over the air. Well, that answered the question if he planned on leaving any time soon.

Turning, she headed into the kitchen, a ridiculously wide grin on her face.

# CHAPTER NINE

Cullen should have left the moment they finished, but he was far from having his fill of her. He wasn't going anywhere. *Maybe ever.*

As soon as the fanciful thought entered, he pushed it away. This wasn't anything but sex. Great sex. But just sex.

She sat close beside him, their thighs touching, as he ate spaghetti in front of the TV. They found a *The Walking Dead* marathon and settled in to watch. He loved looking at her expressive face. Even though she had seen this episode, she still covered her mouth and jumped at all the scary parts.

"So gross! Cannibals." She wrinkled her nose at his bowl of spaghetti. "I'm glad I already ate."

"Ah, c'mon." He held up a marinara-coated meatball. "You don't want a bite?"

"Ick! Get it away." She leaned far to the side, laughing as he pushed his fork at her. "You're going to drop it on me!"

He stuffed it into his mouth. Chewing, he latched onto her waist and tried to kiss her with a mouthful of saucy meatball.

She shrieked and tried to wiggle free. "Stop! Don't!"

He managed to plant a kiss on her cheek, leaving a smear of marina. She wiped it with the back of her hand, laughing.

"Okay, no more," he promised, grinning at her flushed face.

The show came back on and they settled side by side again, offering various opinions.

"I'd be one of the first to go," she said with utter sincerity, shaking her head over her inevitable demise.

"No way. You'd have me, and I'd have explosives."

She laughed and sent him a look. "You know bombs are loud."

"So?"

"Well, that would draw more zombies."

"Not if I kept killing them all," he shot back.

She shook her head, clearly unconvinced at his logic.

"Look," he said. "All I'm saying is that I can rig a bomb with a rubber band and household cleaning products. *And* I can do it fast enough for us to get away."

"Arrogant much?" She snorted.

He shrugged. "I know my strengths."

"Still. I think a tank from the base might be handy to have."

He nodded. "Yeah, except they're gas guzzlers, and I'd imagine we'll have to worry about fuel."

They continued on with their hypotheticals, talking in easy camaraderie until the episode came to an end. It was like every other time they hung out except different. Better. Because there was an easy intimacy between them. He could touch her arm, brush the hair back off her shoulder and she didn't flinch.

"I need a shower," she declared as the next episode started up.

"Go ahead. I'll clean up." He grabbed his plate, feeling her stare on him and fighting the wince. To anyone looking in they would appear almost … domestic. *Hell.*

"Thanks."

He heard the shower water start as he loaded the dirty dishes into the dishwasher. Finished, he turned off the TV and headed for the bathroom. Outside the pink-and-green floral-print shower curtain, he slid off his briefs and pulled the curtain back.

She jumped and yelped like he was one of the zombies they had just finished watching. His gaze dropped, skimming her body. The full breasts with berry-tipped nipples made him instantly hard. He'd had no idea she had such beautiful breasts. Stepping inside the shower, he bent his head and drew one in his mouth. She yelped again, her hands flying to his head. Warm water sluiced over them, making her flesh warm and slippery-sleek in his hands.

He feasted on her breasts, his hand cupping her between her legs, rubbing where she was already wet from a combination of her desire and the shower water.

He backed her into the shower wall, pausing to squirt some body wash into his hands. He brought his hands back to her body, lathering her and massaging everywhere. Breasts, ass, her clenching sex. She closed her eyes, head rolling against the tiled wall. Her blonde hair trailed darkly wet over her shoulders and down her back.

She came, screaming his name, her chest heaving. He lifted one of her thighs, bringing it up to his hip, poised to enter her, but suddenly she broke away and dropped on her knees.

He looked down at her, water sluicing over her. She looked like some sea siren, her ripe mouth at the head of his cock, her blue eyes dark and heavy-lidded, begging for him to ruin her.

She took in his engorged head, rolling it past her lips. She sucked his wet cock into her mouth, as much as she could take. Her slim fingers fisted the base of him that she couldn't swallow. He flattened one hand against the shower wall and fisted his other hand in the wet tangle of her hair.

She sucked him like she would take everything from him. His balls pulled tight and he knew he wouldn't last much longer.

He tried to pull her to her feet. "Huntley, enough."

She ignored him, sucking harder, her free hand coming up to cup his balls. He was lost. He moved his hips, fucking her mouth. She made a moan of approval. Her tongue glided along the underside of his dick, and he was done. He came, losing himself with a cry, and her mouth took all of him, wringing every lost drop from him.

He pulled her up by her arms, feeling dazed. "Huntley."

She stared at him, her eyes glassy, and he knew she felt it, too. That this thing between them was good. Scary good.

She scraped some wet tendrils back from her cheek. "I never really understood why women did that. I never liked it, but that … with you." Her eyes glowed. "I loved it."

His chest squeezed. He brushed a thumb over her cheek and turned her around, finishing washing her body and then himself, his movements brusque, perfunctory. He didn't say another word as they stepped from the shower and dressed again.

It would have made sense to leave after that. To say good night and part ways. They both had work early the following morning. It would have made sense to kiss her goodbye and chalk this up as reckless, crazy hot sex. Instead, he borrowed her toothbrush, flipped off the light and climbed into bed beside her, pulling her close to his side.

He would worry about what made sense later.

* * *

Huntley woke in the dark. She blinked for a moment, knowing something was off. It took another moment for her to remember she wasn't alone. The events of the night flooded over her and her body tingled, deliciously sore and tender from sex. *Sex with Cullen.* Cullen who still slept beside her.

She turned her head, her hand reaching out to touch his bare shoulder. He muttered something and tossed his head, a low wretched sound coming from him. She knew the sound. She had heard the sounds of grief working many a late-night shift in the ER.

"Cullen," she whispered, hoping to ease him from his bad dream. A dream she was certain was rooted in the loss of Xander.

His eyes opened at his name, a soldier accustomed to waking instantly. Pain glazed his eyes. The kind of pain that he never let anyone glimpse during daylight hours. Now with his defenses down, she saw right into him. Through him. He couldn't hide his ghosts from her.

She reached out a hand and stroked his jaw, conveying

that she was here for him. She understood, and she would always be there. He never had to be alone. If he would just let—

He snatched her wrists, tense lines bracketing his mouth. He held her wrists between them, his grip as fierce as his glittering gaze.

She stared back, questioning, unsure. "Cullen, are you all right?"

He dropped his hands from her wrists. His chest rose and fell several times before answering. "I guess I am taking Xander's death hard."

Her pulse skittered at this admission from him. He was talking to her. Actually opening up about what was going on behind his carefully constructed barriers.

"I know."

"I just can't stop wondering what if. What if I had been a better instructor? Halfway through the program Xander came to me expressing doubts. What if I hadn't pushed him to stick with it? I just feel like I failed him. My old man never wanted me to go into EOD." He laughed and the sound was raw with pain. "He said I didn't have the right temperament for it. He said I'd fuck up. I didn't listen to him."

"He was wrong, Cullen. You didn't fail. You did your job." She tossed onto her side to better face him. "Xander was a human being with free will. He made his own choices, and he wouldn't have stuck it out if he didn't want to."

"Yeah, that's my fucking ego, I guess, thinking I matter so much."

"No." Her voice fell hard. "It's not ego. You were his friend. Of course you mattered to him, but you're not God. You weren't responsible for his fate, and I know he's looking down at you now, wanting you to believe that." In the darkness, she could make out the gleam of his eyes as he studied her.

"God, you're too nice. Can there be any girl as sweet as you?"

She frowned. "I'm not sweet."

She'd always been the sweet girl. Predictable. In fact, the only unpredictable thing she ever did was leave Georgia. Of course, she had only done that to get away from Jackson. Everyone assumed they'd get back together. Get married and have the requisite two kids. It was almost as though she feared that happening, so she ran across the country to avoid that fate.

"Sweeter than most girls…" His voice faded, and she knew what he was thinking. *Sweeter than most girls I sleep with.*

She was well acquainted with his normal type of female. Most were Army groupies eager for a meaningless fuck. She wasn't that. This wasn't meaningless for her. He had to know that even without her saying it. He knew her too well.

His hand shifted on her back again, stroking softly. "You deserve so much, Huntley."

"So do you," she countered, her chest aching, almost hurting because she knew he didn't believe that of himself. Especially not carrying the burden of Xander's death. "Some day you'll realize that."

She only hoped it wouldn't be too late before he realized that a part of that better fate he deserved could be a future with her.

"I don't want to hurt you."

"You won't." She touched his face again, and he reached up to hold her wrists.

"You're a good man, Cullen." He needed to hear this. He needed to believe it. He'd been listening to his father call him a fuck-up for years. And now he was blaming himself for what happened to Xander. He needed to know someone believed in him—that *she* did.

He stared at her for a long moment before releasing her wrists. He shoved his hand between her thighs, nudging them apart, sending the question on her lips and her thoughts scattering.

He knuckled her panties aside without a word and plunged a finger inside her. She gasped as he worked her with a few strokes until she was wet.

He withdrew his hand and rolled onto his back, pulling her on top of him. Still holding her panties to the side, he thrust inside her. She cried out, straddling and impaled on him, the sensation tottering the edge of pain and pleasure.

He gripped her waist and guided her with his big hands, practically lifting her up and down until she gained her own rhythm and could move. But even that wasn't enough for him. Not in his present state.

With a growl, he rolled her over onto her knees, hauling her bottom up and pulling her back flush against him. He rubbed his head along her crease, playing in her moist folds for a moment before driving into her again.

She whimpered, an orgasm swelling at the first plunge. Her sex clenched around his thickness. She'd never been taken from behind like this, and the position pushed down on her sweet spot. *OhGodOhGod!* His every thrust stroked along that bundle of nerves and she shuddered, shattering under him.

Her muscles turned to jelly and her body went limp, giving out under him, but he wasn't having it. His grip on her hips tightened and he hauled her back up, holding her for his hammering cock.

One of his hands skated up the slope of her back and curled around her shoulder, anchoring her for him as he fucked her hard. He was a beast. It felt desperate and primal. And she loved it. She was so wet she could hear the slick glide of him working in and out of her. A second orgasm swelled before the tremors from her first had even subsided.

They climaxed simultaneously. He slammed into her with a last grind of his pelvis, his cock pulsing as he released inside her.

Pulling out of her, he dropped down on the mattress. She collapsed onto her stomach, her sex throbbing in the aftermath. She stared wide-eyed into the dark, marveling at how every encounter with him was different, better.

She pressed her fingers to her mouth, holding in any words she might regret.

She would never tire of this, and yet it was ephemeral. As fleeting and illusory as a dream. In the morning it would be gone.

His hand came down on the small of her back, his fingers trailing up the dip of her spine and moving between her shoulder blades. Goosebumps broke out over her skin.

"Did I hurt you?" His deep voice rumbled over the dark, wrapping around her.

"No. I liked it." Loved it. *Loved him.*

*Oh, God.* She wanted to sleep every night beside him. She wanted to be there for him when he woke with a bad dream. His friend. His lover. All of that. She wanted to be everything to him.

She jammed her eyes shut and took a steadying breath,

thankful he couldn't see her face in the dark as she reached this staggering realization.

"I was rough. I'm sorry—"

"I loved it." *I love you.* She exhaled, tapping her fingers against her mouth.

His hand settled flatly on her back, his palm splaying warmly in the center. The imprint of his hand there seared deep into her—through skin, sinew and bone, directly into her soul.

* * *

In the murky light of predawn, Huntley felt the bed dip and shift. All at once she was wide awake. Her heart beat fast in her chest as she stilled and waited, hoping, praying he would kiss her goodbye, maybe whisper a quick promise. She knew he was leaving, but she longed for him to say something. *See you tonight. Call you after work. Let's grab dinner. Can I spend the night again?* Something. Anything but him slipping silently from her room like a thief in the night.

Cracking one eye the barest peep, she identified Cullen's outline at the side of the bed—the broad shoulders and sinewy back tapering to a narrow waist. He moved out of range of vision. She heard the rustle of his clothing and then nothing. She could feel his stare on her in the shadows. A long moment passed.

Her ears strained and her heart locked up inside her at the sound of his tread leaving her room. There was the faint jangle of his keys where he had left them in the living room. The door opening and shutting.

And he was gone.

* * *

He shouldn't have left like that, but it was the kindest thing to do. Much better than putting a brittle smile on his face and making awkward conversation.

He hit the unlock for his truck and slid behind the wheel. They would talk, but first he needed to wrap his head around how this changed everything.

He rubbed at his chest. It felt like a boulder sat there, pressing, pressing.

*You can't give her what she deserves.*

That much was true. He'd promised her brother he would look out for her. Not fuck her until he couldn't remember his own name. And the way he had been with her? *Shit.* The sex had been dirty and rough. The way he liked it.

He pulled out of her driveway and headed for his house. He needed to change before heading to base. He ran three miles every morning with his trainees, and he'd never been late. He glanced at the clock. The guys wouldn't know what to think. Hell, he didn't know what to think.

He dragged a hand over his face and thought about the last ten hours. He'd never had that with a woman before. That closeness, that feeling—both physical and emotional. He wasn't going to pretend he didn't want it again. It was going to be torture to keep his hands off her, to resist her now that he knew how it could be between them.

*So don't resist.*

And what? Be a boyfriend to her? A husband? He didn't do that. Relationships. Monogamy. He wasn't that kind of guy. He was the kind of guy who woke up in sweats from bad dreams. He couldn't be like Beck. He didn't have that seed planted inside him. He failed people. His father. Xander. He made suck-ass decisions. He couldn't trust himself. If he failed Huntley, that would be the deepest cut yet.

Inhaling a deep breath, he vowed to let her go before it got any more complicated than it already was.

# CHAPTER TEN

Two days went by before Huntley saw Cullen again.

He'd sent her a text the previous night explaining they had night drills. She knew they occasionally conducted training exercises that simulated wartime scenarios. That he thought to text her at all should have mollified her, but it did little to quell the ache of not seeing him or alleviate the tangle of her thoughts churning in aimless circles in an effort to figure out what they were to each other now.

She texted him back and invited him over on Friday night. Beck and his new girlfriend were coming over for dinner. Kenna would be going back to Georgia with him, and Beck had decided to stay a little longer and help her pack her things.

Cullen had texted back that he would join them but might be running late. She glanced at the door all through dinner, wondering if he really was going to make an appearance.

He finally arrived when she was serving dessert, his hair still damp from a shower. She inhaled his soapy scent and the faint whiff of deodorant as he passed her into the dining area, and all her girl parts quivered with longing, eager for an encore.

"Hey, man." Beck rose and clapped him on the back, pulling him close in one of those half hugs guys did. He motioned to Kenna. "This is Kenna. My girl."

Even Cullen smiled over Beck's dreamy tone as he grasped Kenna's extended hand. "Nice to meet you.

Cullen's gaze lifted back to Huntley and a giddy tingle spread throughout her.

"I can cut a piece of lasagna for you," she offered. "Or would you like a piece of cake?"

Cullen's gaze slid over her, warming her everywhere. "I'll have a slice of cake."

Desire slicked through her, tightening her skin. Her bones felt like pudding beneath his gaze. Why did it feel like he was asking for something else?

"A cup of coffee, please, too, if you have it."

Nodding, she turned and disappeared inside her small kitchen that suddenly felt too cramped and hot. She told herself it was overly warm from the lasagna she had baked for two hours, but the oven had been off for more than an hour now. Her hands shook as she fetched a mug from the cabinet.

When she turned, she yelped, nearly dropping the mug in her hands to find him directly behind her.

"Sorry," he murmured, his shoes thudding on the tile floor as he stepped close, so close she could count the tiny flecks of gold in his brown eyes. He didn't look sorry. No, the directness of his gaze said a lot of things, but it wasn't an apology.

"S'kay," she murmured, palming the smooth mug in her hand. The counter's edge cut hard into her back. He didn't seem in any hurry to step aside for her. "You just startled me."

"A little jumpy?" His eyes scanned her face.

She shook her head and then nodded, undecided on what she was, but figuring it was okay to admit the truth. She was jumpy around him, and standing this close made her feel like she was coming out of her skin.

Stepping forward to pass around him, she sucked in a breath as her front brushed the hard wall of his chest. Lust shot through her. Even though she wore a blouse. Even though he wore a soft cotton T-shirt. Her breasts tightened, the tips reacting on memory, pinching into tight, needy points.

A hiss of breath escaped him. At the sound, a steady calmness came over her. He felt it, too. He wanted her again.

She turned her back to him, slicing into the chocolate cake she had baked yesterday when she was going out of her mind thinking about him and needing a distraction. She cut four generous slices, setting each one down on a dessert plate. She covered the cake with the glass dome with one hand, lifting an icing-coated finger to her lips. Before she could lick her finger clean, Cullen's long fingers wrapped around her wrist.

He leveled a searing gaze on her, intent and hungry for something that definitely was not cake. Her chest squeezed so tightly it ached. She watched him, her eyes wide, as he lifted her hand to her mouth. He brought her index finger into his mouth, sucking the chocolate-coated fingertip. She gasped and his eyes darkened. He made a low growling sound of satisfaction. Her stomach dipped and twisted as he circled her finger with his tongue, licking off every last bit of icing.

"Need help with the cake, sis?" Beck called from the other room.

She jumped guiltily at the sound of her brother's voice. Mortification fired her cheeks as she thought about him in the next room. Her brother walking in on her getting her finger sucked by his best friend wasn't exactly on her things-to-do list. She pulled her finger free and hastily collected three plates. Eyes still trained on her, Cullen picked up the last plate of cake and followed her out of the kitchen, only to find Beck and Kenna locked in a scorching kiss that made her want to spoon out her eyes. As much as she adored her brother, there were some things you just didn't want to see.

She cleared her throat and they withdrew from each other, both looking like they wished they were alone in a bedroom and not in her kitchen. She could understand that. Her finger still tingled from Cullen's mouth, and that wasn't the only part of her tingling.

She passed around the cake.

"Mmm, delicious," Kenna said after taking her first bite.

"Hunt knows her way around a kitchen," Beck volunteered.

She shrugged self-consciously. "Well, Grandma didn't let me leave Georgia without copying down all her recipes."

Her brother nodded at Cullen. "Surprised Hunt didn't fatten you up while I was gone, Cullen."

Cullen dug into a huge mouthful of cake that would have been four bites for her. "If I didn't run so much, she would have."

They finished their cake in silence. Plate empty, Beck leaned back in his chair, his fingers trailing in the ends of Kenna's dark strands. "Have you given any more thought to what we talked about, Huntley?"

She felt the weight of Cullen's gaze on her and shifted uneasily. "A little," she replied vaguely, knowing he was referring to her moving back to Georgia.

"It'd be nice to have you near us." Her brother draped his hand over Kenna's bare knee. For a moment his gaze got lost there, like that pretty knee was all he wanted in this world. Huntley risked a quick glance up to find that Cullen was watching her with almost equal intensity.

She quickly escaped his stare, looking back at her brother and Kenna. They were an "us" now. A lump formed in her chest. She was happy for him ... and envious.

"Talk to her, Cullen." Beck tore his gaze off Kenna's knee and clapped Cullen on the shoulder. "Tell her she should move back home."

A flicker of something passed over Cullen's face. Huntley held her breath, trying to read him, to decipher what it was she had seen there in that split second.

"I don't know," Cullen answered slowly. "She should do what she wants. Do you want to move back home?" Air deflated from her lungs as Cullen lifted an eyebrow at her.

"Well, Hunt? What do you want to do?" Beck prodded.

She moistened her lips, her gaze stuck on Cullen. "I—I don't know."

Cullen's gaze dropped to his cake, cutting another bite as if her answer didn't matter one way or the other to him. "I guess you better decide that first."

The next half hour passed in a miserable blur. What had

she expected? For Cullen to declare himself? Announce that he loved her and needed her here? That kind of thing only happened in movies. Not. Her. Life.

After accepting two slices of chocolate cake to go, Beck and Kenna left.

Cullen made himself at home, busying himself in the kitchen, loading dishes into the dishwasher like it was any other night they were hanging out.

*Why couldn't they have this all the time? Well, with the added bonus of sex, of course.*

She watched him for a moment, crossing her arms and leaning against the counter, admiring the way his jeans fit. God. How could she ever be in the same room with this man and not want to crawl inside him? Loading the last glass, he shut the dishwasher door and turned. His mouth curled up at one corner as he caught her watching him. "Hey."

"Hey," she rejoined. "You didn't have to do that. You didn't even dirty the majority of them."

"I don't mind. And I fully intend to take some lasagna home with me."

So he wouldn't be staying the night then?

She moved into the living room and sank down on the couch, tucking her legs beneath her and willing the awkwardness between them to evaporate. She reached for the remote as he lowered beside her, glad to have something to occupy her hands.

"Want to watch some TV?" She tried not to stare at his muscled thighs or the way his shirt rested against his flat stomach and cut pecs. "I think there's a *Vikings* marathon on." She barely made it to the right channel before warm fingers circled her ankle.

She gasped and dropped the remote as he tugged her foot onto his lap. "What are you doing?" she choked.

"Rubbing your feet. You've been on them all day."

She sighed in joy the moment his thumbs pushed down on the balls of her feet. Her body went limp and she melted into the couch. He was right. She had been on her feet all day. Even with the best shoes and massaging gel-cushioning inserts, her feet ached by the end of her shift. "That is amazing."

His eyes smiled down at her as the heel of his hand glided along her arch, exerting the perfect amount of pressure. Her feet wept for joy, but that wasn't the only part of her reacting. Pleasure radiated from her feet and traveled up her legs, settling between her thighs. A low throb pulsed there as he cupped her heel and ground down on the flesh with the pad of his thumb. Sensation shot to every nerve in her body.

"Ohhhh, your hands are amazing," she moaned.

His grin deepened. "I've been told."

She tossed one of the smaller couch cushions at his face. "I bet."

They fell into companionable silence, the awkwardness of earlier gone. She turned her face into the couch to stifle another moan. When his hands glided up her calves and started working into the tense flesh, she was lost. Her knees turned to pudding, falling slightly open in invitation.

"Huntley?"

"Hmm?"

"We need to talk."

She frowned. She didn't want to talk. Not right now. She just wanted him to keep doing delicious things to her with his hands. Maybe he could add his mouth next. She wouldn't be opposed to him unsnapping his jeans either and taking out—

"Huntley?" he pressed. "Last night ..."

Dread pooled in her. Nothing good would follow those words, she was sure.

"It was good," he continued, his thumb tracing circles on the inside of her leg. Her heart tripped inside her chest.

*Good?* She snorted. That's all it was to him? She pulled her legs away, tucking her knees against her chest.

"But?" she said, her tone sharper than she intended. She propped her chin on her knees. "I can hear the 'but' in there. Is this where you let me down easy? You don't have to do that, Cullen. I know you. I'm not one of your other women you have to evade."

"Other women?" His gaze narrowed on her face, the softness of his mouth disappearing as his lips hardened into an unsmiling line. "What are you talking about?"

"We're friends who just happened to sleep together. I get that. You don't have to worry that I'll want something more from you."

He leaned back on the couch, tossing his arm along the back in a casual pose that felt anything but casual despite his calm tone. "You done?"

She nodded once, uncertain at his tone of voice.

He continued, "So that's it then? We just had a romp in the sheets and it's out of our system now?"

She nodded again, her uncertainty growing.

"I see," he said, looking away, his gaze falling on the TV.

"We're still friends. We'll always be—"

"Friends," he inserted, looking at her sharply. "That's

what you want?"

She held his gaze, no longer certain of anything. "You don't want that?"

"You're asking now, Huntley? Sounds like you have this all figured out. But hey, you're moving back home. Right?" The words hung between them, a challenge waiting a response.

"Uh. I'm considering it." *What the hell was she saying? She wasn't leaving. She liked her life here.*

"Well, it makes sense to keep things casual. Just fucking for fucking's sake."

"Right," she murmured, staring blindly at the TV, wondering why his words felt like such a slap to the face.

The ringtone of her phone jarred the silence between them. She grabbed it off the coffee table and answered it without looking to see who was calling, glad for the sudden distraction.

"Hey, Huntley, it's Greg. How are you doing?"

Cullen tensed beside her and she knew he could hear Greg's voice.

"Uh, fine. How are you?" He'd sent her a few texts since their coffee date. She replied to one or two but ignored most of them. She couldn't even imagine seeing him again. Even if her heart wasn't invested in Cullen, they weren't a good match.

She snuck a glance at Cullen's face, not hearing a word Greg was saying as she eyed him. His jaw was locked and his gaze drilled into her, bright and intense. There was a look in his eyes that reminded her of him at the coffeehouse when he had watched her with Greg. A dark little thrill raced through her as she remembered how that night had ended.

"Mm-hm," she murmured to whatever Greg was saying. Something about another date.

Cullen inhaled sharply and she knew he could hear every word. She winced. *God.* She wasn't trying to make him jealous. Truly. And he had no reason to feel jealous. They weren't in an exclusive relationship. Her feminine hackles rose even as some other part of her wakened and trembled, craving his hands on her again. His body hard and strong, taking over hers and making her want things she never knew she wanted.

She gave her head a small shake and tightened her fingers around the phone, getting off on that glint in Cullen's eyes that warned her he was close to losing it.

He stood from the couch and stopped before her, his belt buckle on level with her eyes. She gulped and flicked her gaze up to his face. Eyes like flint.

His hands circled her ankles and yanked her until she was flat on her back on the couch. She gasped into the phone.

"You okay, Huntley?" Greg asked into her ear.

"Yeah, I'm fine." She squeaked as Cullen slid his big hands up her legs.

He leaned down and bit the lobe of her ear, sending a sharp spike of lust through her at the pleasure-pain. "You're more than fine," he growled. "Why don't you tell him you're about to get fucked hard and deep by me. Again."

She moaned. Her body reacted on a primitive level—sex tingling, breasts growing heavy with need.

"Huntley? Are you okay?" Greg asked worriedly as Cullen's breath fanned hotly in her ear. A rush of moisture soaked her panties.

"Y-yes," she choked. "I have to g-go."

The words were barely out of her mouth before Cullen plucked the phone from her hand and tossed it aside.

His deep voice purred near her face. "No sense in stringing him along. You're not going out with him again."

She opened her mouth … to say what, she wasn't certain. She didn't want to go out with Greg. That was true.

His chest lifted on a ragged breath. "Right now you're mine."

How dare he act so high-handed? A roaring rush filled her ears. She didn't think. Just reacted. She lashed out, punching him in the chest. Not a flicker of pain crossed his face. He didn't even flinch.

He bent over her, his voice lethal. "Hit me if it makes you feel better. I can take it." His dark eyes glinted and she knew he meant it. Maybe it even got him off a little.

Inhaling, she told herself anger at this situation was her most dominant emotion, but she knew that was a lie. Hunger stirred within her.

She moaned his name as he slid off her leggings in one move and flipped her over on the couch.

His broad hand smoothed over the rounded swell of her ass. "Not his. You got that?" His hand came down on her with a smack. She jolted at the contact, moaning low in her throat as a bolt of heat shot straight between her legs. She dipped her spine and arched her bottom higher in the air, asking for more, wishing her panties were gone, her anger from moments ago melting into air.

She trembled on all fours as he ran a hand up her thigh and slid it over her stinging cheek, giving her a hard squeeze before knuckling aside her underwear. With the same hand he cupped her sex, massaging it until all ability to speak fled her.

"This is mine," he growled.

Her head swam. They had just established this was merely sex between them. *This is mine.* He didn't mean it. It was just one of those things people said during sex. Passionate words blurted out during the throes. Sullen Cullen never stuck with any single female.

The ability to think vanished as he slid a finger inside her. She bowed her spine, thrusting her bottom in the air, drawing him in deeper.

His lips landed on her bared cheek, kissing her where he had spanked her. "Say it." His voice rumbled against her, vibrating from somewhere deep in his chest.

"I'm not saying that."

He bit down, his teeth sharp and punishing on her tender skin. She cried out and to her utter bewilderment, moisture rushed between her legs, edging her toward orgasm.

He slowed the pumping action of his finger between her legs, his mouth talking against the skin he just bit. "Your body says it loud and clear. You just got real wet for me, sweetheart." His mouth traveled up to the small of her back, tender kisses dragging over her goose-puckered flesh. "Say it," he commanded.

The tenderness got to her. She panted heavy breaths into the couch cushion, thrusting her bottom up at him, urging his finger to continue its assault. "I'm yours."

His thumb pressed down hard on her clit in reward and she flew apart, coming in a muffled shriek, arms clutching the couch cushion, her fingers digging into the fabric. Her knees trembled, threatening to give out.

Cullen slipped his finger free. "There you go, sweetheart."

She heard the faint sing of his zipper over the crashing of her breath. He grabbed her hips in both hands, hoisting her up. "Grab the back of the couch," he commanded.

She folded her fingers over the hard edge, still fuzzy-headed from her orgasm.

A hissing breath escaped her as she felt the plump head of his cock at her opening. He dragged the tip up and down her crease, grazing it over her sensitive clit.

"Oh, God," she moaned.

He pushed in, just the head of him. "You feel that, sweetheart?"

She nodded and sounds passed her lips that might have resembled speech but sounded like something an animal would make.

He pushed in a little deeper and she whimpered. The walls of her channel stretched, fighting to accommodate him.

"You won't forget me. No one is ever going to touch you like this. No one will make you come like I can. No ex-boyfriend. No other man."

A sob welled up in her chest. He was already assuming she was gone. He was okay with that.

He didn't give her time to adjust or catch her breath. He thrust deep, filling her. Seizing her hips, he hammered into her, leaning low, covering her back with his chest. His big hands slid beneath her tunic top, cupping her breasts as he worked in and out of her. His agile fingers tugged the lacy cups of her bra down until her breasts bobbed above the bunched fabric. He fondled the heavy, aching flesh, his fingers playing over her nipples until they pebbled hard.

She started pushing back against him, meeting the thrust of his cock, slamming her ass against him, wanting to punish him for talking to her like she was gone. He growled, his fingers pinching harder on her nipples, snapping some invisible cord that held her together. Sensation swelled through her, starting at her sex and rolling out all the way to her toes.

He chuckled, low and deep, the sound rasping against her nape. "That's right." He slipped a hand between them, rolling the tender nub of her clit. "Who owns this?"

She shrieked, convulsing against him, hating and reveling in his utter arrogance. As her orgasm ebbed and faded, she let go of the couch and squeezed out from under him, fully aware that he had yet to reach his climax.

"Huntley, what—"

She turned and pushed him back down on the couch, her palms flat on his chest as she straddled him, wrapping a fist around him and guiding him back inside her. She sank down on him, a huff of breath escaping her at feeling him like this. Impaled upon him. She had never felt a man so deep and hard. Not that she had a wealth of experience to draw from, but it was almost like he was reaching up into her heart. Truly a part of her. If this was to be their last time, then she intended for him to remember her.

His hands dropped to her waist. He gripped her, ready to move her up and down, but she wasn't having it. She seized his wrists and pushed them up by his head. She locked gazes with him and held herself still over him.

"What are you doing, Huntley?"

"It's *my* turn."

Heat flared in his eyes. "Then start moving."

She shook her head at him. "You've had your way. It's my turn to do this my way."

"Your turn? You've gotten off twice. I'd say it's my turn now."

Bending her head, she bit him on his pec. He made a short sound, part growl, part moan, as her inner muscles tightened around him.

"Feel that?" she asked, loosening her fingers around his wrists.

His hands came down and smoothed over the rounded swells of her ass. "Yeah." He croaked, his fingers digging and flexing on her in a way that made her ache and clench around him again.

She framed his face with her hands and kissed him slow and deep, her tongue tasting, stoking the kiss until it became something hot and wild between them.

Her sex continued to pulse and squeeze around his cock as the kiss grew feverish and intense. He tried to move his hips and she broke the kiss, pushing a hand down hard on his chest, pinning him to the couch. "You don't move," she reprimanded.

"Fuck," he gasped. "I have to move."

The desperate words were almost her undoing. Her inner muscles worked, squeezing, wringing his cock, eager for increased friction and pressure.

He arched his throat on a moan. "I feel that. You want it, too. Let me go."

"I set the pace." She shifted, easing out a fraction and then coming down and seating herself fully, grinding on him and rocking her pelvis.

Leaning down, she kissed his throat, inhaling his scent, scoring the taut skin with her teeth. She trailed kisses all over his throat and collarbone, loving the salty taste of his skin.

At his ear, she bit down on the lobe and lifted her hips, treating him to another slow and easy pump.

A hoarse, broken cry was her reward. As she came back down, she squeezed tight around his hard length, gasping at the friction. His fingers dug into her hips, hanging onto her like his life depended on it. His head rolled side to side on her couch, sweat beading his forehead. She had never felt so empowered—or so utterly feminine.

His jaw clenched, a muscle feathering the taut flesh of his cheekbone. She fanned her fingers against his cheek, kissing him and savoring his mouth before sliding her lips along his square jaw in a flurry of kisses.

"Huntley," he begged in a voice she had never heard from him. From any man. Arching, she began to rock her hips, moving above him sinuously, sinking down slowly and dragging back up. She reached a hand around her and cupped his balls, squeezing them gently in her fist.

He surged up, his hips lifting her as he came in a guttural cry, releasing himself deep inside her, his fingers digging so firmly on her hips she knew she would bear marks later.

He collapsed back down, his face slack with pleasure, eyes closed. His beautiful chest slick with perspiration.

She dropped over him, their bodies glued to each other, breathing as one.

"As far as fucking goes, that might have been … the best." His voice gusted over the top of her head.

She smiled, supremely satisfied with herself. "I might have to agree." Her fingers rested on the hard plane of his stomach, tapping lightly.

His voice rumbled over the air. "I'm going to miss this."

Her satiated smile slipped at the drop of his words.

*Why the hell had he gone and said that?*

Did he find it necessary to remind her that this wasn't permanent? That it couldn't be lasting? She hesitated for a moment before pulling away. Without looking at him, she snatched up her top and pulled it over her head, not bothering with a bra.

"What's wrong?" he asked.

She looked at his face, not quite meeting his eyes. "Nothing." As she slipped on her panties, her gaze grazed over him on her couch. Every gorgeous inch of him that wasn't hers. She blinked against the sudden burn in her eyes.

He propped up on his elbows, watching her closely. "You just went from hot to cold in ten seconds flat. Is it what I said?"

"No. It's nothing."

Nothing except that he seemed eager for her to move back to Georgia. It would make all of this easier. Give whatever this was between them an end date.

She stepped into her leggings, her movements stiff with anger.

His dark eyes narrowed. "Let's not bullshit each other here. If you're angry say it."

"Fine. I'm angry." She planted both hands on her hips, feeling liberated at admitting it.

"Really? You're mad?" He shot up off the couch, standing in front of her without a care in the world for his nakedness. "Because you're the one talking about moving right after we started sleeping together. I'm not the one leaving."

She stared at him, outrage washing over her. "Beck and my family want me to move back. I—I haven't decided."

"Any why not?" he accused. "Why haven't you

decided, Huntley?"

This was it. The moment she could declare herself and say: *I'm not going. I'm staying because of you.* Just a few words, but they terrified the hell out of her and stuck like a golf ball lodged in her throat. What if he didn't feel the same way about her?

She squared her shoulders, her pride surfacing. Why couldn't *he* say it? Nothing was stopping him. Why did it have to be here? Why did she have to take the risk?

Cullen watched her, unblinking, his eyes fastened on her face. His naked chest lifted on a breath and his eyes cut her like glass, dark as night waters. "Maybe you should just go."

The words cut, burrowing deep. She watched his face carefully. Nothing. His expression was impassive.

"Maybe I should." The words tumbled out of her, a stupid mistake the minute she said them and yet she couldn't take them back.

They stared. After a long moment, he turned, grabbed his shirt off the floor and tugged it over his head. He snatched up his briefs and jeans next. "You need to do what's right for you, Huntley. What makes you happy."

The words weren't issued with any heat. There was no anger in them. On the contrary, he actually said them kindly. Magnanimously. But they still felt like the cruelest jab.

He didn't care.

She nodded stiffly. She wanted him to be selfish. To demand she stay for him.

Her chest hurt, the ache there so intense, so stabbing and profound. Like nothing she had known when she and Jackson broke up.

He nodded. "Let me know if you need any help moving."

She sucked in a deep breath. That was the final nail in the coffin. He had actually offered to help her pack. This guy did not want her around. At least not badly enough to try and persuade her to stay.

She blinked burning eyes and turned her attention to tidying up the couch cushions.

Why did they have to sleep together? Sex always ruined everything. At least friendships. If they had kept their hands off each other, she wouldn't now be facing a move. A pang punched her in the chest and she rubbed at her breastbone, her fingers massaging the tender area.

"Will do," she replied through suddenly numb lips, not bothering to correct his misapprehension that she was moving. It didn't matter. He was out of her reach.

He nodded once, brusque, turned for the door, and stepped out into the night.

As soon as the door clicked shut, she dropped down on the couch. Dry sobs sucked in and out of her. She pressed one hand against her chest and closed her eyes in a long blink. Was there any choice in the matter? The moment Cullen made his move, her heart and body were his. Logic stood no chance. The fallout was unavoidable.

She lifted her chin and stared unseeingly ahead. Unseeing and yet seeing. She would live in close proximity to Cullen. She'd cope. Hopefully, they could still be friends.

Maybe someday they would even look back and laugh over their fling. She winced. It was hard to imagine that now, but maybe.

She'd stay here. This was her life. Her home. Even if Cullen wasn't a part of it.

# CHAPTER ELEVEN

Cullen stormed into his house and flung his keys against the wall. He dropped down on his couch and scrubbed both hands over his face before standing and pacing a hard line in his living room.

Had he actually offered to help her pack?

*Fuck, fuck, fuck.*

The knock at his door pulled him up hard. He stared at it for a long moment, then his heart kicked into gear, pounding like a drum. *Huntley.*

In two strides he yanked open the door and stared at Beck standing there.

"Beck," he said numbly, his heart deflating.

With a tight smile, his friend walked into the house. He looked around before facing Cullen.

"It's late," Cullen said rather dumbly. "What are you doing here?" From his last glimpse of Beck, he didn't think the guy would pry himself off Kenna until well into next week, but here he was. Alone.

"I figured you would be back from Huntley's by now," he finally said.

Cullen watched his friend closely. He hadn't left Huntley's until a good while after Beck and Kenna bailed.

"Yeah?" He scratched the back of his head, tension hovering between them. As Cullen stared down Beck, he was hard pressed not to think about what he had been doing to Beck's sister just a short while ago … and harder pressed not to feel guilty about it.

"Yeah." Beck nodded once. "Thought it was time we talked about what's going on between you and Hunt."

Everything inside of Cullen locked tight in battle-readiness. He stared at Beck warily as he circled the living room. "What do you mean?"

Beck smiled humorlessly. "C'mon, man. It's obvious you're sleeping with my sister." He shrugged one massive shoulder. "That wasn't exactly what I had in mind when I asked you to look after her, but if you're going to treat her with the respect she deserves, then we won't have a problem. She's an adult who makes her own decisions. A fact my girlfriend might have mentioned several times on the ride home."

Cullen exhaled, not about to lie or deny the allegation. He knew touching Huntley had broken a code, but he wasn't sorry for it. In fact, the only thing he regretted at the moment was how things went down between them back at her house.

Beck arched a brow and looked pointedly at Cullen. "So. Do we have a problem?"

Cullen shook his head and dropped back down on his couch. "She's going back to Georgia."

Beck studied him a moment. "Is that a fact?"

Cullen nodded once.

"And you're down with that plan?"

"It's her decision. I can't make her stay here if she doesn't want—"

Beck threw back his head and laughed. "Are you really that stupid? You have to give her a reason to stay. Same way I gave Kenna a reason to go. Have you asked Hunt to stay at Black Rock?"

Cullen's hands opened and closed into fists. Was it that easy? He simply had to ask? "Maybe it's best if she goes." He dragged a hand over his head. "I only know that I can't let her down." He failed his father. He failed Xander. He couldn't fail Huntley, too.

"Maybe you don't want her to stay," Beck challenged. "Maybe you had your fun with her and now you're done."

"*Hey.*" Cullen surged to his feet, forgetting for a moment that this was Huntley's brother. He grabbed Beck by the front of his shirt and shook once. "It's not like that."

"No? Then what is it like?" At Cullen's silence, Beck nodded. "Maybe you need to figure that out before she's gone. Because my sister is strong and she'll move on, while you're sitting here, wondering how the hell you let her get away." He moved for the door and pulled it open. "Think about that."

Thinking about that was all he did for the rest of the night.

He didn't sleep a wink, staring into the dark, wondering when he had become so thoroughly fucked. He'd fallen in love with his best friend and had done everything wrong … everything to send her packing and walking out of his life forever.

It dawned on him then.

The exact thing he didn't want to happen—failing Huntley, losing her—was happening.

*Shit.* If he didn't fix things with Huntley now, it would be too late.

Maybe it already was.

* * *

"There's a patient complaining of chest pains in exam room five," Nancy, the senior nurse on duty, said as Huntley walked up to the nurse's station after assisting one of the doctors with a broken arm in exam room three. She'd seen it time and time again. Alcohol and foosball did not mix.

Huntley eyed the clock, eager for when she could take her break and grab a latte from the food truck outside. "And I'm guessing you want me to take the patient?"

"You don't mind, do you?"

"Course not." Busy was good. Busy stopped her from thinking too much about Cullen. When she returned to her empty house tonight, she would have plenty of time for that.

Huntley took the chart and started down the hall, stopping when something occurred to her. She looked over her shoulder. "Exam room five?"

The other nurse shrugged, smiling mysteriously as she drifted in the opposite direction down the hall. Chest pain was usually prioritized into exam rooms one or two. Unless triage had deemed the patient low priority for some reason.

She continued, pushing open the door, a greeting on her lips as she flipped open the chart, ready to glance over the patient's basic information—and found it blank.

Huntley looked up, her heart stopping at the sight of Cullen sitting on the exam table. Her chest squeezed at the sight of him. Those molten chocolate eyes. The hard body unmistakable beneath his fatigues. He braced his hands on each of his thighs in an anxious manner.

"Cullen? What are you doing here?"

*Cullen was here. In front of her.*

She snapped shut the chart, knowing she had been sabotaged. A quick glance up and down his lean body confirmed that he looked as hale and hearty as ever. He had to get Nancy's help for this. "Shouldn't you be at work?" she demanded.

He placed a hand over his heart. "I hurt. Right here."

Her lips twitched at the utter seriousness of his expression. "That so?"

Pulse racing, she set the chart down on the counter and walked forward. Clearing her throat and ignoring the sudden constricting of her own heart, she feigned seriousness. "When did this pain start?"

"A few nights ago."

"I see." She swallowed against the sudden dryness of her throat and resisted the urge to fling her arms around his neck. "Can you describe the pain?"

He nodded solemnly. "Yeah, at first my pulse raced and it felt like my heart might explode."

"Hm. Interesting."

"And then last night, the pain changed."

"Yeah?"

"Yeah." His hands closed around her hips, hauling her between his thighs. She suddenly didn't think she was the only one whose heart might explode. "When you started talking about moving back home, leaving Black Rock, leaving me … it felt like a knife was stabbing me right here." He took her hand and placed it over his heart. His eyes crawled over every inch of her face, his gaze penetrating past skin and bone, burrowing deep into her soul. "It still does."

"Oh," she breathed, her too-tight chest lifting, trying to pull in air. She supposed she could tell him she had no intention of moving. Maybe later. After he said everything he came here to say.

"Oh," he echoed. "There's only one way to make it stop. Only one way to fix me."

She moistened her lips. "Well, then tell me. I'm a nurse. It's my responsibility to—"

He silenced her with a kiss, his mouth slanting and moving on hers until she forgot whatever it was she was meant to say. He pulled back, leaving her gasping, his hand cupping her cheek. "Stay."

"W-what?" Her voice trembled from her lips, but it was nothing compared to the way her heart shuddered inside her chest.

"I need you to stay. To live here. With me." His fingers tightened over hers. "I need you to love me back."

Her heart overflowed at those words. "Cullen," she choked. "You love me?"

"I love you. I always have. I just didn't know. You're in my blood, Huntley. If you go, I'm lost."

She nodded jerkily, blinking, trying not to cry. "I'm not going anywhere. I never intended to. This is my home."

Relief flashed across his face. "Well, that's good to know."

"As far as loving you," she continued. "I do. I have.

For a long time."

He brought his other hand up, framing her face in both hands. "So. Are you moving into my place, or am I moving into yours?"

She laughed. "Isn't that a little sudden? A little bit—"

"Sweetheart, we've been dating for years. We just didn't realize it." He smiled, but his eyes drilled into her—intense, solemn. "And I don't want to spend another night without you."

"Wow," she breathed. "You don't waste time."

"I know what I want." His thumb traced her mouth. "And all this time we could have been having sex."

"We have a lot of catching up to do," she agreed, bringing her other hand up to his chest, reveling in the hardness of his flesh beneath her palm and hating the clothes barring her from complete access.

"Why don't we get a new place together?" he suggested, kissing her jaw, her throat, inching toward the collar of her scrubs. "A fresh start for both us?"

"We might as well." She nodded in approval.

"Some place big enough for all the kids we're going to have."

"Kids?" Her heart jumped wildly in her chest. She tugged his face back up.

"Well, yeah, we'll get married first, of course. But there will be babies, Huntley."

Tears burned in her eyes; there was no stopping them. She wiped at her cheeks with the back of her hand. She tried to speak, but a broken sob escaped instead.

"This isn't very romantic, is it?" He frowned as if the idea just occurred to him. "Proposing this way. I should have—"

"It's perfect." She sniffed, her fingers curling into his shirt, gripping hard. "It's beautiful. It's you. I wouldn't want anything different."

"I won't fail you." He smoothed a hand over her hair.

"I know you won't."

"I'll try to give you everything, Huntley."

"Just love me."

"Done." He kissed her again, slow and deep and forever.

an be obtained
om

6

TESSA lives in Brooklyn, New York with her husband and young daughter. When she isn't writing or reading romance, Tessa enjoys a good argument and thirty-minute recipes. Find out about new releases from Tessa at **www.tessabailey.com**

**Line of Duty Series**

*Protecting What's His*

*Protecting What's Theirs*

*His Risk To Take*

*Officer Off Limits*

*Asking For Trouble*

*Staking His Claim*

**Crossing the Line Series**

*Riskier Business*

*Risking It All*

**Serve Series**

*Owned By Fate*

*Exposed By Fate*

*Driven By Fate*

**Broke and Beautiful Series**

*Chase Me*

*Need Me*

**Standalone Titles**

*Unfixable*

*Baiting The Maid Of Honor*

SOPHIE lives in Houston, Texas with her husband and children. When she isn't writing or reading romance, Sophie enjoys lattes and cramming her DVR with shows she watches after her kids go to bed. Find out about new releases from Sophie at **www.sophiejordan.net**

**The Ivy Chronicles**

*Foreplay*
*Tease*
*Wild*

**Young Adult Romance**

The *Firelight* Trilogy
(*Firelight*, *Vanish*, And *Hidden*)
*Uninvited*
*Unleashed*

**Historical Romances**

*Once Upon A Wedding Night*
*Too Wicked To Tame*
*One Night With You*
*Surrender To You*
*Sins Of A Wicked Duke*
*In Scandal They Wed*
*Wicked Nights With A Lover*
*How To Lose A Bride In One Night*
*Lessons From A Scandalous Bride*
*Wicked In Your Arms*
*A Good Debutante's Guide To Ruin*

CPSIA information
at www.ICGtesting.
Printed in the USA
FFOW03n05050702
21119FF